"The only dessert I want is a taste of your sweet lips."

"Yes." London breathed the word and it came out sounding almost like a plea.

"Are you sure it's not too forward of me?"

Harrison seemed determined to tantalize and torment her with what could be. The suggestion of a kiss did exactly what it was supposed to. It frustrated her and aroused her curiosity at the same time. She reached up and tunneled her fingers into his hair.

"Kiss me like you want to," she urged.

"If I do that we might get arrested." His husky laugh puffed against her skin, making her shiver.

Annoyed at the ache pulsing through her and how easily he'd aroused it, London lay her palm against his chest. The chemistry sparkled between them, ripe with promise and potential.

"I don't know what to do with you," she murmured, trembling as he drew her tight against his hard body.

"Funny," he said. "I know *exactly* what to do with you."

* * *

Substitute Seduction is part of the Sweet Tea and Scandal series from Cat Schield.

Dear Reader,

I'm excited to bring you the second book in my Sweet Tea and Scandal series set in historic Charleston, South Carolina. When I originally conceived a trilogy about three women taking revenge on the men who wronged them, I knew London McCaffrey needed a man who could muss up her perfect exterior and wake the passion slumbering in her.

Enter race-car driver Harrison Crosby, the hot and sexy brother of the man she's supposed to be taking down. I love this couple's chemistry and their opposites-attract story line.

As always, Charleston makes a wonderful backdrop for the romances playing out among the city's elite. The historic homes, fantastic restaurants and local flavor capture the heart of what makes the South so fascinating. So grab a glass of sweet tea, and I hope you enjoy this scandalous romance.

Happy reading,

Cat Schield

CAT SCHIELD

SUBSTITUTE SEDUCTION

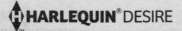

HARLEQUIN® DESIRE

Recycling programs
for this product may
not exist in your area.

ISBN-13: 978-1-335-97187-6

Substitute Seduction

Printed in U.S.A.

Cat Schield has been reading and writing romance since high school. Although she graduated from college with a BA in business, her idea of a perfect career was writing books for Harlequin. And now, after winning the Romance Writers of America 2010 Golden Heart® Award for Best Contemporary Series Romance, that dream has come true. Cat lives in Minnesota with her daughter, Emily, and their Burmese cat. When she's not writing sexy, romantic stories for Harlequin Desire, she can be found sailing with friends on the Saint Croix River, or in more exotic locales, like the Caribbean and Europe. She loves to hear from readers. Find her at catschield.net and follow her on Twitter, @catschield.

Books by Cat Schield

Harlequin Desire

Las Vegas Nights

At Odds with the Heiress
A Merger by Marriage
A Taste of Temptation
The Black Sheep's Secret Child
Little Secret, Red Hot Scandal
The Heir Affair

Sweet Tea and Scandal

Upstairs Downstairs Baby
Substitute Seduction

Visit her Author Profile page at Harlequin.com, or catschield.net, for more titles!

Prologue

"We need to get back at all of them. Linc, Tristan and Ryan. They need to be taught a lesson."

When Everly Briggs had decided to attend the Beautiful Women Taking Charge event, she'd researched the attendees and settled on two women she believed she could convince to participate in a devious plot to take down three of Charleston, South Carolina's most influential men.

Each of the three women had shared a tale of being wronged. Linc Thurston had broken his engagement to London McCaffrey. Zoe Crosby had just gone through a brutal divorce. But what Ryan Dailey had done to Everly's sister, Kelly, was by far the worst.

"I don't know about this," London said, chewing on

her coral-tinted lip. "If I go after Linc, it will blow up in my face."

"She's right." Zoe nodded. "Anything we try would only end up making things worse for us."

"Not if we go after each other's men," Everly said, pierced by a thrill as her companions started to look hopeful. "Think about it. We're strangers at a cocktail party. Who would ever connect us? I go after Linc. London goes after Tristan and, Zoe, you go after Ryan."

"When you say 'go after,'" Zoe said hesitantly, "what do you have in mind?"

"Everyone has skeletons in their closet. Especially powerful men. We just need to find out where the worst ones are hiding and let them out."

"I'm in," London said. "Linc deserves to feel a little pain and humiliation for ending our engagement the way he did."

Zoe nodded. "Count me in, too."

"Marvelous," Everly said, letting only a small amount of her glee show as she lifted her glass. "Here's to making them pay."

"And pay," London echoed.

"And pay," Zoe finished.

One

The party celebrating the ten-year anniversary of the Dixie Bass-Crosby Foundation was in full swing as Harrison Crosby strolled beneath the Baccarat crystal-and-brass chandelier hanging from the restored ante-bellum mansion's fifteen-foot foyer ceiling. Snagging a glass of champagne from a circling waitress, Harrison passed from the broad foyer with its white marble floor and grand columns toward the ballroom, where a string quartet played in the corner.

Thirty years ago Harrison's uncle Jack Crosby had purchased the historic Groves Plantation, located thirty-five miles outside the city of Charleston, intending to headquarter Crosby Motorsports on the hundred-acre property. At the time, the 1850s mansion had been in terrible shape and they'd been on the verge of knocking it down when both Virginia Lamb-Crosby and Dixie Bass-Crosby—Harrison's mother and aunt respectively—had raised a ruckus. Instead the Crosby family had dumped a ton of money into the historic renovation to bring it up to code and make it livable. The result was a work of art.

Although Harrison had attended dozens of charity events supporting his family's foundations over the years, the social whirl bored him. He'd much rather just donate the money and skip all the pomp and circumstance. Despite the Crosby wealth and the old family connections his aunt and mother could claim, Harrison had nothing in common with the Charleston elite and preferred his horsepower beneath the hood of his Ford rather than on the polo field.

Which was why he intended to greet his family, make as little small talk as he could and get the hell out. With only three races left in the season, Harrison needed to stay focused on preparations. And he needed as much mental and physical stamina as possible.

Spying his mother, Harrison made his way toward her. She was in conversation with a younger woman he didn't recognize. As he drew near, Harrison recognized his mistake. His mother's beautiful blonde companion wore no ring on her left hand. Whenever his mother encountered someone suitable, she always schemed to fix him up. She didn't understand that his racing career took up all his time and energy. Or she did get it and hoped that a wife and family might persuade him to give it all up and settle down.

Harrison was on the verge of angling away when

Virginia "Ginny" Lamb-Crosby noticed his approach and smiled triumphantly.

"Here's my son," she proclaimed, reaching with her left hand to draw Harrison in. "Sawyer, this is Harrison. Harrison, I'd like you to meet Sawyer Thurston."

"Nice to meet you," Harrison said, frowning as he tried to place her name. "Thurston..."

"Linc Thurston is my brother," Sawyer clarified, obviously accustomed to explaining about her connection to the professional baseball player.

Harrison nodded. "Sure."

Before he could say anything more, his mother reinserted herself into the conversation. "Sawyer is a member of Charleston's Preservation Society and we were just talking about the historic home holiday tour. She wants to know if I'd be willing to open the Jonathan Booth House this year. What do you think?"

This was the exact sort of nonsense that he hated getting involved in. No matter what his or anyone else's opinion, Ginny Lamb-Crosby would do exactly as she liked.

He leaned down to kiss her cheek and murmured, "I think you should ask Father since it's his house, too."

After a few more polite exchanges Harrison pretended to see someone he needed to talk to and excused himself. As he strolled around the ballroom, smiling and greeting those he knew, his gaze snagged on a beautiful woman in a gown of liquid sky. Her long honeyed hair hung in rolling waves over her shoulders with one side pulled back to show off her sparkly dangle earring. In a roomful of beautiful women, she stood out to him because rather than smiling and enjoying herself, the blonde with big eyes and pale pink lips wore a frown. She seemed to barely be listening to her chatty companion, a shorter, plump brunette of classic beauty and pouty lips.

She seemed preoccupied by... Harrison followed her gaze and realized she was staring at his brother, Tristan. This should have warned Harrison off. The last thing he wanted to do was to get tangled up with one of his brother's castoffs. But the woman inspired more than just his curiosity. He had an immediate and intense urge to get her alone to see if her lips were as sweet as they looked, and that hadn't happened in far too long.

Turning his back on the beauty, he headed to where his aunt was holding court on one side of the room near a large television playing a promotional video about the Dixie Bass-Crosby Foundation. In addition to helping families with sick children, the foundation supported K–12 education programs focused on literacy. Over the last ten years, his aunt had given away nearly ten million dollars and her family was very proud of her.

Yet even as Harrison exchanged a few words with his aunt, uncle and their group, his attention returned to the lovely blonde in the blue dress. The more he observed her, the more she appeared different from the ladies who normally appealed to him. Just as beautiful, but not a bubbly party girl. More reserved. Someone his mother would approve of.

The more he watched her, the more he labeled her as uptight. Not in a sexual way, like she wouldn't know an orgasm if it reached out and slapped her, but in a manner that said her whole life was a straitjacket. If not for her preoccupation with Tristan, he might've turned away.

He simply had to find out who she was, so he went in search of his uncle. Bennett Lamb knew where all the bodies were buried and traded in gossip like other men bought and sold stock, real estate or collectibles.

Harrison found the Charleston icon holding court near the bar. In black pants and a cream honeycomb dinner jacket with a gold bow tie and pocket square, Bennett outshone many of the female guests in the fashion department.

"Do you have a second?" Harrison asked, glancing around to make sure his quarry hadn't escaped.

One of Bennett's well-groomed eyebrows went up. "Certainly."

The two men moved off a couple of feet and Harrison indicated the woman who'd interested him. "Do you know who that is?"

Amusement dancing in his eyes, his uncle gazed in the direction Harrison indicated. "Maribelle Gates? She recently became engaged to Beau Shelton. Good family. Managed to hold on to their wealth despite some shockingly bad advice from Roland Barnes."

Harrison silently cursed at the word *engaged*. Why was she so interested in Tristan if she was unavailable? Maybe she was cheating on her fiancé. Wary of letting his uncle think he'd shown an interest in someone who was engaged, he asked, "And the brunette?"

"Maribelle Gates is the brunette." Bennett saw where his nephew was going and shook his head. "Oh, you were interested in the blonde. That's London McCaffrey."

"London." He experimented with the taste of her name and liked it. "Why does her name ring a bell?"

"She was engaged to Linc Thurston for two years."

"I just met his sister." Harrison returned to studying London.

Meanwhile his uncle kept talking. "He recently broke off the engagement. No one knows why, but it's rumored he's been sleeping with…" Bennett's lips curved into a wicked grin. "His housekeeper."

An image of the heavyset fifty-year-old woman who maintained his parents' house popped into Harrison's mind and he grimaced. He pondered the willowy blonde and wondered what madness had gripped Linc to let her go.

"He doesn't seem the type to go after his housekeeper."

"You never know about some people."

"So why is everyone convinced that he's sleeping with her?"

"*Convinced* is a strong word," his uncle said. "Let's just say that there's speculation along those lines. Linc hasn't been out with anyone since he and London broke up. There's been not a whisper of another romance on anyone's radar. And, from what I hear, she's a young widow with a toddler."

Harrison shoved aside the gossip and refocused on the object of his interest. The more Bennett speculated about the reason Linc Thurston had for ending the engagement, the less he liked London's interest in his brother. She deserved better. Tristan had always treated women poorly, as his recent behavior during his divorce from his wife of eight years demonstrated. Not only had Tristan cheated on her the entire time they were married, he'd hired a merciless divorce attorney, and Zoe had ended up with almost nothing.

"Now, if you're looking for someone to date, I'd like to suggest…"

Harrison tuned out the rest of his uncle's remarks as he continued to puzzle over London McCaffrey. "Is she seeing anyone at the moment?" Harrison asked, breaking into whatever it was his uncle was going on about.

"Ivy? I don't believe so."

"No," Harrison said, realizing he hadn't been paying attention to whatever pearls of wisdom his uncle had been shelling out. "London McCaffrey."

"Stay away from that one," Bennett warned. "That mother of hers is the worst. She's a former New York socialite who thinks a lot of money—and I do mean a lot—can buy her way into Charleston inner circles. Honestly, the woman is a menace."

"I'm not interested in dating the mother."

"London is just as much a social climber," Bennett said as if Harrison was an utter idiot not to make the connection. "Why else do you think she pursued Linc?"

"Obviously you don't think she was in love with him," Harrison retorted dryly.

He wasn't a stranger to the elitist outlook held by the old guard of Charleston society. His own mother had disappointed her family by marrying a man from North Carolina with nothing but big dreams and ambition. Harrison hadn't understood the complexities of his mother's relationship with her family and, frankly, he'd never really cared. Ever since he could remember, all Harrison had ever wanted to do was to tinker with cars and drive fast.

His father and uncle had started out as mechanics before investing in their first auto parts store. Within five years the two men had parlayed their experience and drive into a nationwide chain. While Harrison's dad, Robert "Bertie" Crosby, was happy to man the helm and expand the business, his brother, Jack, pursued his dream of running race cars.

By the time Harrison was old enough to drive, his uncle had built Crosby Motorsports into a winning team. And like the brothers before them, Tristan had gone into the family business, preferring to keep his hands clean, while Harrison loved every bit of oil and dirt that marked his skin.

"She pursued him," Bennett pronounced, "because her children would be Thurstons."

Harrison considered this. It was possible that she'd judged the guy by his social standing. On the other hand, maybe she'd been in love with Linc. Either way, Harrison wasn't going to know for sure until he had a chance to get to know her.

"Why are you so interested in her?" Bennett asked, interrupting Harrison's train of thought.

"I don't know."

He couldn't explain to his uncle that London's preoccupation with Tristan intrigued and worried him. For the last couple of years Harrison had increasing concerns about his brother's systematically deteriorating marriage to Zoe. Still, he'd ignored the rumors of Tristan's affairs even as Harrison recognized his brother had a dark side and a ruthless streak.

The fact that Zoe had vanished off his radar since she'd first separated from Tristan nagged at Harrison. In the beginning he hadn't wanted to get involved in what had looked to become a nasty divorce. Lately he was wishing he'd been a better brother-in-law.

"Do you know what London does?" Harrison asked, returning his thoughts to the beautiful blonde.

Bennett sighed. "She owns an event planning service."

"Did she plan this event?" An idea began to form in Harrison's mind.

"No. Most of the work was done by Zoe before…" Not even Bennett was comfortable talking about his former niece-in-law.

"I think I'm going to introduce myself to London McCaffrey," Harrison said.

"Just don't be too surprised when she's not interested in you."

"I have a halfway-decent pedigree," Harrison said with a wink.

"Halfway decent isn't going to be enough for her."

"You're so cynical." Harrison softened his statement with a half smile. "And I'm more than enough for her to handle."

His uncle began to laugh. "No doubt you're right. Just don't be surprised when she turns you down flat."

* * *

London McCaffrey stood beside her best friend, Maribelle Gates, her attention fixed on the tall, imposing man she'd promised to take down in the next few months. Zoe Crosby's ex-husband was handsome enough, but his chilly gaze and the sardonic twist to his lips made London shiver. From the research London had done on him these last couple of weeks, she knew he'd ruthlessly gone after his wife, leaving her with nothing to show for her eight-year marriage.

In addition to cheating on Zoe through most of their marriage, Tristan Crosby had manufactured evidence that she was the one who'd been unfaithful and violated their prenuptial agreement. Zoe had been forced to spend tens of thousands of dollars disproving this, which had eaten into her divorce settlement. A settlement based on financial information about her husband's wealth that indicated he was heavily mortgaged and deeply in debt.

Zoe's lawyer suspected that Tristan had created offshore shell companies that allowed him to hide money and avoid paying taxes. It wasn't unusual or illegal, but it was a hard paper trail to find.

"Heavens, that man cleans up well," Maribelle remarked, her voice breathy and impressed. "And he's been staring this way practically since he arrived." She nudged London. "Wouldn't it be great if he's interested in you?"

With an exasperated sigh, London turned to her friend and was about to reiterate that the last thing on her mind was romance when she recognized the man in question. Harrison Crosby, Tristan's younger brother.

A racing-circuit fan favorite thanks to his long, lean body and handsome face, Harrison was, to her mind, little more than a glorified frat boy. Zoe had explained that her ex-brother-in-law liked fast cars, pretty women and the sorts of activities that red-blooded American males went for in the South.

"He's not my type," London told her best friend, returning her focus to her target.

"Sweetie, I love you," Maribelle began, settling further into her native South Carolina drawl, "but you have to stop being so picky."

Resentment rose in London but she studiously avoided showing it. Since the first time her mother had slapped her face for making a fuss during her sixth birthday party, London had decided if she was going to survive in the McCaffrey household, she'd better learn to conceal her emotions. It wasn't always easy, but now, at twenty-eight, she was nearly impossible to read.

"I'm not being picky. I'm simply being realistic." And since he wasn't the Crosby brother she was targeting, he wasn't worth her time.

"That's your problem," Maribelle complained. "You're always realistic. Why don't you let loose and have some fun?"

Out of kindness or sympathy for her longtime friend, Maribelle didn't mention London's latest failure to climb the Charleston social ladder. She'd heard more than enough on that score from her mother. When London had begun to date someone from one of Charleston's oldest families, her mother had perceived this as the social win she'd been looking for since the New York socialite had married restaurant CEO Boyd Mc-Caffrey and moved to Connecticut, leaving her beloved New York City behind. And then, when London's father had been accepted for a better position and moved his family to Charleston, Edie Fremont-McCaffrey's situation grew so much worse.

When she'd first arrived, Edie had assumed that her New York connections, wealth and style would guarantee Charleston's finest would throw open their doors for her. Instead she'd discovered that family and ancestral connections mattered more here than something as vulgar as money.

"It's not that I don't want to have fun," London began. "I just don't know that I want to have Harrison Crosby's sort of fun."

Well, didn't that make her sound like the sort of dull prig who'd let the handsome and wealthy Linc Thurston slip through her fingers? London's heart contracted. Although she no longer believed herself in love with Linc, at one point she'd been ready to marry him. But would she have? London wasn't entirely clear where their relationship would be if he hadn't broken things off.

"How do you know what sort of fun Harrison Crosby likes?" Maribelle asked, bringing London back to the present.

She bit her lip, unable to explain why she'd been researching the Crosby family, looking for an in. There were only three people who knew of their rash plan to take revenge on the men who'd wronged them. What

London, Everly and Zoe were doing might not necessarily be illegal, but if they were discovered, retribution could be fierce and damaging.

"He's a race-car driver." As if that explained everything.

"And he's gorgeous."

"Is he?"

London considered all the photos she'd seen of him. Curly black hair, unshaved cheeks, wearing jeans and a T-shirt or his blue racing suit with sponsor patches plastered head to toe, he had an engaging smile and an easy confidence that proclaimed he had the world on a string.

"I guess if you like them scruffy and rough," London muttered. Which she didn't.

"He looks pretty suave and elegant to me."

Maribelle's wry tone spiked London's curiosity and she carefully let her gaze drift in his direction. Not wanting the man to think she was at all interested in him, she didn't look directly at him as she took in his appearance.

The Harrison Crosby she'd been picturing looked nothing like the refined gentleman in a perfectly tailored dark gray suit that drew attention to his strong shoulders and narrow hips. Her hormones reacted with shocking intensity to his stylish appearance. He was clean-shaved tonight, appearing elegant enough to have stepped off a New York runway. Where she'd been able to dismiss the "rough around the edges good ol' boy" in racing attire, London saw she'd miscalculated the appeal of a confident male at the top of his game.

"Apparently he cleans up well," London remarked

"Not your thing?" he guessed, demonstrating an ability to read the subtle currents beneath her answer.

"She mostly organizes corporate and charity events," Maribelle responded with a sweet smile that stabbed at London's heart.

"Oh, that's too bad," Harrison said, the impact of his full attention making London's palms tingle. "My brother's turning forty next month and I was going to plan a party for him. Only I don't know anything about that sort of thing. I don't suppose you'd like to help me out?"

"I…" Her first impulse was to refuse, but she'd been looking for an opening that would get her into Tristan's orbit. Planning his birthday party would be an excellent step in that direction. "Don't usually do personal events, but I would be happy to meet with you and talk about it."

She pulled a business card out of her clutch and handed it to him.

He glanced at the card. "'London McCaffrey. Owner of ExcelEvent.' I'll be in touch." Then, with a charming smile, he said, "Nice meeting you both."

London's eyes remained glued to his retreating figure for several seconds. When she returned her focus to Maribelle, her friend was actively smirking.

"What?"

"See? I told you. What you need is a little fun."

"It's a job," London said, emphasizing each word so Maribelle wouldn't misinterpret the encounter. "He's looking for someone to organize his brother's birthday party. That's why I gave him my card."

"Sure." Maribelle's hazel eyes danced. "Whatever you say. But I think what you need is someone to take your mind off what happened between you and Linc, and in my not-so-humble opinion, that—" she pointed at the departing figure "—is the perfect man for the job."

Everything London had read about him stated that he liked to play hard and that his longest relationship to date had lasted just over a year. She'd decided her next romance would be with a man with a serious career. Someone she'd have lots in common with.

"Why do you think that?" London asked, unable to understand her friend's logic. "As far as I can tell, he's just like Linc. An athlete with an endless supply of eager women at his beck and call."

"Maybe he's just looking for the right woman to settle down with," Maribelle countered. She'd been singing a different tune about men and romance since she'd started dating Beau Shelton. "Can't you at least give the guy a chance?"

London sighed. She and Maribelle had had this conversation any number of times over the last few months as her friend had tried to set her up with one or another of Beau's friends. Maybe if she said yes Maribelle would back off.

"I'm really not ready to date anyone."

"Don't think of it as dating," Maribelle said. "Just think of it as hanging out."

Since London was already thinking in terms of how she could use Harrison to get to Tristan, it was an easy enough promise to make. "If it means you'll stop bugging me," she said, hiding her sudden satisfaction at killing two birds with one stone, "I'll agree to give Harrison Crosby one chance."

Two

Harrison spent more than his usual twenty minutes in the bathroom of his penthouse condo overlooking the Cooper River as he prepared for his meeting with London McCaffrey.

A woman he'd dated for a short time a year ago had given him pointers on grooming particulars that women appreciated. At the time he'd viewed the whole thing with skepticism, but after giving the various lotions, facial scrubs, hair-care products and other miscellaneous items a try, he'd been surprised at the results and happily reaped the benefits of Serena's appreciation.

Still, as much as he'd seen the value in what she'd introduced into his life, his focus during racing season left little room for such inconsequential activities. Today, however, he'd applied all that he'd learned, scrutinizing

ExcelEvent logo painted in white on the gray wall. "She shouldn't be too long."

"Thank you."

Ignoring the couch, Harrison stood in the center of the room, wondering how long she would leave him cooling his heels. While he waited, he took stock of his surroundings, getting a sense of London's taste from the clean color palette of black, white and gray, the hint of drama provided by the silver accessories and the pop of color courtesy of the flower arrangement on the reception desk. On the wall across from him was a large-screen TV with a series of images and videos from various events that London had organized.

In his hand, his phone buzzed. Harrison sighed as he glanced at the message on the screen. Even though he took Mondays and Tuesdays off during the season, rarely an hour went by that his team wasn't contacting him as they prepared the car for that week's upcoming race. Each track possessed a different set of variables that the teams used to calibrate the car. There were different settings for shocks, weight, height, springs, tires, brakes and a dozen other miscellaneous factors.

For the first time in a long time, Harrison debated leaving the text unanswered. He didn't want to split his focus today. His team knew what it was doing. His input could wait until his meeting with London concluded.

A change in the air, like a fragrant spring breeze, pushed against his skin an instant before London McCaffrey spoke his name.

"Mr. Crosby?"

As he looked up from his phone, Harrison noted the

his hands to ensure they were grease-free and [...]
his nails more than a cursory clipping, even go[...]
far as to run a file over the edges to smooth awa[...]
sharpness. Although he didn't touch the high-tech [...]
cars until he slid behind the wheel, Harrison often [...]
wound from a race weekend by tinkering with the [...]
classics his uncle bought for his collection.

Today, however, as he surveyed his charcoal jeans, g[...]
crewneck sweater and maroon suede loafers, Harrison [...]
cided that someone as stylish as London would appreci[...]
a man who paid attention to his grooming. And in trut[...]
his already elevated confidence was inflated even furth[...]
when the receptionist at ExcelEvent goggled at him as [...]
strolled into the King Street office.

"You're Harrison Crosby," the slender brunette ex[...]
claimed, her brown eyes wide with shock as he advance[...]
on her desk. "And you're here." She gawked at him, he[...]
hands gripping the edge of the desk as if to hold herself in place.

Harrison gave her a slow grin. "Would you let London know I've arrived?"

"Oh, sure. Of course." Never taking her eyes off him,
she picked up her phone and dialed. "Harrison Crosby is
here to see you. Okay, I'll let him know." She returned
the handset to the cradle and said, "She'll be out in a
second. Would you like some coffee or water or...?" She
trailed off and went back to staring at him.

"I'm fine."

"If you want to have a seat." The receptionist gestured to a black-and-white floral couch beneath the

uptick in his heartbeat. Today she wore a sleeveless peach dress with a scalloped neckline and hem, and floral pumps. Her long blond hair fell over her shoulders in loose waves. Feminine perfection with an elusive air, she advanced toward him, her hand outstretched.

Her fingers were cool and soft as they wrapped around his hand. "Good to see you again."

"I intend to call you London," he said, leaning just ever so slightly forward to better imprint the faint scent of her floral perfume on his senses. "So you'd better call me Harrison."

"Harrison." Still holding his hand, she gazed up at him through her lashes, not in a manner he considered coy, but as if she was trying to take his measure. A second later she pulled free and gestured toward a hallway behind the reception desk. "Why don't you come back to my office?" She turned away from him and led the way, pausing for a brief exchange with the receptionist.

"Missy, were you able to get hold of Grace?"

"I had to leave a message. Do you want me to put her through when she calls?" Missy glanced at Harrison as she asked the question.

"Yes. It's urgent that I speak with her as soon as possible." London glanced back at Harrison as she entered her office. Like the reception area, this tranquil space was decorated in monochrome furniture and accessories. "I hope you don't mind the interruption, but I'm organizing a fiftieth wedding anniversary for a client's parents in a week and some things have come up I need her to weigh in on. She's currently out of the country and not due back until just before the party."

"I understand." His phone vibrated with another in-coming text as if to punctuate his point. "I'm sure you have all sorts of balls in the air."

"Yes." She gestured him toward a round table to their left and closed the door. "I always have several projects going at once."

"Are you a one-woman show?" His gaze tracked her as she strode to her glass-topped desk and picked up a utilitarian pad and basic pen. No fancy notebooks and expensive writing instruments for London McCaffrey.

"No, I have several assistants," she explained as she sat across from him. "Most of them help me out on a part-time basis, but I have two full-time employees plus Missy, my receptionist."

"I didn't realize your company was so large."

She acknowledged the implied compliment with a slight smile. "I've been fortunate to have expanded rap-idly since I opened my doors."

"How long have you been in business?" Harrison leaned back in his chair and let his gaze flow over her slender shoulders and down her bare arms.

She sat forward, arms resting on the tabletop, the pen held lightly in her fingers. "Nearly six years. I started right out of college."

"Why an event planning company?"

Her eyes narrowed as if she'd suddenly noticed that he was interviewing her, but her voice remained smooth and unruffled as she answered. "My mother used to be a socialite in New York and has always been big on the charity circuit. I started attending events when I was in my teens and mostly found them tedious because I didn't know anyone. To keep myself occupied, I would spend my time analyzing the food, decor and anything else that went into the party. When I got home, I would write it all down and make notes of what I would do differently."

Harrison found himself nodding in understanding as she described her process. "That sounds a lot like how I got into car racing. My uncle used to let me help him work on the cars and, when I got old enough to drive, gave me the opportunity to get behind the wheel. I could tear apart an entire engine and put it back together by the time I was fourteen."

"I guess we both knew what we wanted to do from an early age."

"Something we have in common." The first of many somethings, he hoped.

As if realizing that they'd veered too far into the personal, she cleared her throat. "So you said you were interested in having someone organize a party for your brother's birthday?"

"Yes." Harrison admired her segue back to the reason for his visit. "He turns forty next month and I thought someone should plan something."

After meeting London the other night, Harrison had called his mother and confirmed that no one was in the process of planning anything for Tristan's fortieth birthday. In the past, events like this had been handled by Tristan's wife, Zoe, but she was out of the picture now.

She tapped her pen on the notepad. "Tell me something about your brother."

Harrison pondered her question for a moment. What

did he know about Tristan? They were separated by more than just an eight-year age difference. They had different ideologies when it came to money, women and careers. Nor had they been close as kids. Their age differences meant the brothers had always attended different schools and Tristan's free time had been taken up by sports and friends.

"He runs the family business since our dad semi-retired five years go," Harrison began. "Crosby Automotive is a billion-dollar national chain of auto parts stores and collision centers in twenty states. We also have one of the largest private car dealership groups on the East Coast."

"And you race cars."

Her matter-of-fact tone carried no judgment, but Harrison imagined someone as no-nonsense as London McCaffrey wouldn't view what he did in a good light. No doubt a guy like Tristan, who put on an expensive suit and spent his days behind a desk, was more her cup of tea. On the other hand, she had been engaged to a baseball player, so maybe Harrison was the one guilty of being judgmental.

"I'm one of four drivers that races for Crosby Motorsports."

"Car twenty-five," she said, doodling a two and a five on her legal pad before encircling the numbers with a series of small stars.

He watched her in fascination. "Yep."

"I've never seen a race." She glanced up, caught him watching her and very quickly set the pen down atop the drawing as if embarrassed by her sketch.

"Well, you're in luck," he said. "I'm racing on Sunday in Richmond."

"Oh, I don't think…" Her eyes widened.

"It's my last race of the season." He made his tone as persuasive as possible.

London shook her head. "It's really not my thing."

"Then what is?"

"My thing?" She frowned. "I guess I don't really have one. I work a lot, you see."

"And that leaves no room for fun?"

"From what my friend told me about a racer's schedule, I'd like to know when you slow down for fun."

"You have me there. I'm on the go most of the year."

She nodded as if that put an end to the topic. "So, how many people are you looking to invite to your brother's birthday party?"

"Around a hundred." He'd secured a list from his mother after realizing he'd better not show up to a party planning meeting empty-handed and clueless.

"And do you have a budget?" London had relaxed now that they'd returned to familiar territory and flipped to a clean page so she could jot notes.

"Keep it under ten."

"Thousand?" She sounded a tad surprised, leaving Harrison questioning whether he'd gone too high or too low. "That amount opens up several possible venues. Of course, the timing is a little tight with it being the start of the holiday season. Did you have a particular date in mind?"

"His birthday is December fifth."

"I'll have Missy start calling around for availability." She excused herself and went to speak to her receptionist.

Harrison barely had a chance to look at any of the several texts that had come in while they'd been talking before she returned.

"Are you thinking a formal sit-down dinner with cocktails before and dancing afterward or something more casual?"

"My mother insists on a formal event. But I don't think dancing. Maybe a jazz band, giving people a chance to mingle and chat." Harrison was even more relieved that he'd checked with his mother because he was able to parrot everything she'd suggested.

"You were smart to get her input," London said, picking up on his train of thought. "I guess my last question for now is whether you had any sort of theme in mind."

Theme? Harrison was completely stumped. "I guess I was just thinking it was his fortieth birthday…"

"A color scheme?"

More and more Harrison wished he'd found a different way to connect with London McCaffrey. "What would you suggest?"

Her lips pursed as she pondered the question. "I'll pull together three ideas and run them past you. What are you thinking about for the meal?"

"Wouldn't it depend on the place we choose?"

"Yes, but it might help narrow things down if I thought you wanted seafood versus steak and chicken."

"Ah, can I think about it?"

With a slight shake of her head, she pressed on. "Give me your instant thoughts."

"Seafood."

She jotted that down. "There are several venues that do an exceptional job."

Although he'd never planned an event like this before, Harrison was finding that the process flowed easily with London in charge. She was proving to be both efficient and knowledgeable.

"You're really great at this," he said.

Her lips quirked. "It is what I do for a living."

"I didn't mean to sound surprised. It's just that I've never thrown anyone a birthday party before and you're making everything so easy."

"If you don't mind my asking, how did you come to be in charge of this particular event?"

Harrison doubted London was the sort who liked to play games, so he decided to be straight with her. "I volunteered because I was interested in getting to know you better and a friend warned me that you wouldn't be inclined to give me a shot."

"Get to know me better?" She looked more curious than annoyed or pleased. "So you decided to hire me to plan your brother's birthday party? You should know that I don't date my clients."

Despite her claim, he sensed she wasn't shutting him down entirely. "You said you usually work with corporate clients. Maybe this would be an excellent opportunity to gain some exposure with Crosby Automotive. And I get a chance to work with a woman who intrigues me. A win-win solution all around."

Interest colored her voice as she echoed, "A win-win solution…"

* * *

London's pen flowed across the legal pad as she randomly sketched a centerpiece and pondered Harrison's words.

When he'd called to set up this meeting, she'd been elated. Organizing his brother's birthday party would solve the problem of how she could get close enough to Tristan to figure out how to bring him down. The more she learned about Zoe's ex-husband, the more daunting her task. Frustration welled up in London as she considered the impulsive bargain she'd made several months earlier. What had she been thinking to agree to something that could lead to trouble for her in the future if she wasn't careful? But how did she back out now that Everly and Zoe had their plans in motion?

"Would you like to have dinner with me tonight?" Harrison asked.

The abruptness of his invitation combined with the uptick in her body's awareness of him caught her off guard, and London was shocked and dismayed by the delight blooming in her.

"I…"

She'd been so focused on her goal of helping Zoe that she hadn't considered the possibility of an interpersonal relationship between her and Harrison. Now, with his startling confession, the situation had grown complicated.

"Ever since meeting you at the party the other night, I can't stop thinking about you," he declared, his sea-toned eyes darkening as his voice took on a smoky quality. "You don't date your clients, but there's nothing that says you can't. Let me take you to dinner."

You made this devil's bargain. Now see it through.

"Tomorrow would be better," she responded a touch breathlessly.

"I'm heading to Richmond with the crew tomorrow. Tonight is all I have."

She was on the verge of refusing when his smile faded. An intense light entered his eyes and London found it difficult to breathe. The man's charisma was off the charts at the moment and London found herself basking in the glow of his admiration. At the same time she couldn't help but wonder if he was sincere or merely plying her with flattery to get her into bed. Worse, she wasn't sure she cared.

Maribelle's words came back to haunt her. London could use a little fun in her life and rebound sex with Harrison Crosby might be what enabled her to move on from Linc. If only she wasn't planning to use Harrison as part of their revenge plot.

"I don't want to have to wait another week to spend an evening with you," he continued as she grappled with her conscience.

"I'm flattered," she said, stalling for time.

His lips kicked into a dry grin. "No, you're not."

Harrison wasn't the sort of Southern gentleman she was used to. One she could wrap around her finger. He had a straightforward sex appeal that excited her and made her feel all needy and prone to acts of impulsiveness. The urge to grab his sweater and haul him over for a kiss shocked her.

"Really—" Her instincts screamed at her to retreat. Her susceptibility to this man could prove dangerous.

"You think I'm hitting on you because I want to sleep with every woman I meet."

"I wouldn't dream of thinking such a thing," she murmured in her most guileless drawl as she glanced down at her legal pad and noticed she'd been drawing hearts. She quickly flipped to a clean page and set down her pen.

"Don't go all Scarlett O'Hara on me," Harrison replied. "I'm not going to lie and tell you I don't see us ending up in bed, but I fully intend on making it about the journey and not the destination."

Outrage poured through London, but there was a certain amount of amusement and curiosity mixed in, as well. Damn the man. His plain speaking was having the wrong sort of effect on her.

"You seem pretty sure of yourself," she said. "What makes you think I'm interested in you that way?"

"The fact that you're still here discussing it with me instead of kicking me to the curb."

"Do you honestly think you're the first client who has hit on me?"

"I'm sure I'm not." He didn't look at all concerned by her attitude. "But I'm guessing you're going to give me a different answer than all the others."

It pained her that he was right. Nor could she console herself with the falsehood that she would turn him down flat if it wasn't for this pact she'd made with Zoe and Everly.

"I'll have dinner with you tonight," she said. "But I get to pick the place and I'll meet you there."

"And I promise to behave like a proper gentleman."

She snorted. "There's nothing proper or gentlemanly about you, I think." A delicious shiver worked its way down her spine at the thought. "Do you agree to my conditions?"

"If they make you feel safe, then how can I not?"

His use of the word *safe* made her bristle. She hadn't set conditions because of any nervousness she felt around him, but to make him understand that she wasn't one of those women who flatter and swoon all in the hope of achieving that elusive five-carat sparkler for their left hand.

"How about we meet at The Front Porch at eight o'clock."

"That's perfect."

She then steered the conversation back to the original reason for their meeting. "It would be a good idea if we could meet next week and check out a couple of the venues," she told him, already having a pretty good idea of the sort of elegant evening she intended to organize.

"I'll be back in town next Monday and Tuesday."

She picked up her phone and pulled up her calendar. "I'm open Monday afternoon, say two o'clock? The faster we book a location, the sooner we can start working on the details. And I'll pull some ideas together and send them along to you this week."

"Sounds great."

They'd arrived at an obvious end to their meeting and Harrison stood. As London escorted him to the front door, he asked, "Are you sure you wouldn't want to come watch me race in Richmond?"

London's eyes flicked to her receptionist. Missy was paying rapt attention to their exchange without actually staring at them. Heat bloomed beneath London's skin as she realized that word would soon spread about Harrison's invitation.

"I don't know…"

"You could bring your friend. Maribelle, wasn't it?"

"Yes." To her dismay, London's mood had dipped at the thought of sharing his attention. "I mean, yes, my friend is Maribelle. She's a huge fan. Both her and her fiancé, Beau."

"Bring them both along. I'll get you seats in our suite."

London considered how enthusiastic her friend had been after meeting Harrison. It surprised her that someone who had been trained from birth to epitomize a gracious Southern lady had an interest in such a loud and tedious sport. All the drivers did was go around and around in circles at high speeds for three hours. How could that possibly keep anyone interested?

"I'll see if she's busy and let you know." The words were out before London could second-guess herself.

She needed access to Tristan, and Harrison was the perfect way in. From the way her pulse triggered every time he smiled at her, acting interested wouldn't be a problem. She just needed to be careful that she kept her body's impulses in check and her mind focused on the revenge bargain.

Harrison looked a little surprised that she'd changed

her mind, but then a grin slowly formed on his face. "Great."

"Wonderful," she murmured, reaching out to shake his hand.

She'd begun the gesture as a professional event planner, but as his long fingers enveloped hers, a jolt of electricity surged up her arm. The raw, compelling reaction left London wobbly. She couldn't let herself be distracted right now. Not when she had a mission and Harrison played an integral part in accomplishing it.

Capitalizing on his interest in her was one thing. Reciprocating the attraction would only lead to trouble.

"See you at eight."

Aware that they were still holding hands, London pulled her fingers free. "Eight," she echoed, glad Harrison had the sense not to gloat as she opened the front door and gestured him onto the sidewalk. "In the meantime, I'll keep you informed as we confirm availability on the potential venues."

After they said goodbye, she wasted no time watching him walk away, but immediately turned to her receptionist. Seeing that Missy was making a poor effort at busywork, London gathered herself to scold her and then realized if she'd been worried about the scene playing out in front of an audience, she should've taken him outside.

"Let me know what you hear from the venues," she said, heading for her office.

With a whoosh of breath, she plunked down on her office chair and ignored the slight shake in her hands as she jiggled the mouse to deactivate her screensaver.

However, as she struggled to refocus on what she'd been working on before Harrison had shown up, peeling her thoughts away from the handsome race-car driver proved challenging.

Unsure what to make of his confessed interest in her and invitation to dinner tonight, she contemplated her legal pad and the mixture of notes and doodles. No fewer than ten hearts lined the margins and swooped across the page. What had she been thinking?

London opened a file on her computer for the event and typed in her notes before tearing the page into tiny pieces.

Going forward she needed to take a firmer grip on her subconscious or heaven only knew what might happen.

Once her initial work on the fortieth birthday party was done, London dialed Maribelle to give her a heads-up about all that had transpired and to extend Harrison's invitation to watch him race on Sunday.

"Beau will be thrilled," Maribelle said. "Do you think Harrison can get us into the pit on race day?"

"Maybe. I can find out what that entails." She traced her fingertips over the twenty-five she'd once again doodled on her legal pad. At least there were no hearts this time. "We're having dinner tonight."

Maribelle's squeal forced London to pull the phone away from her ear. "See, I knew he was interested in you. Where are you going? Is he taking you somewhere romantic? Are you going to sleep with him? I would. I bet he's great in bed. He's so sexy with that dark hair and those blue-green eyes. And that body. I read that he's in crazy great shape. What I wouldn't give to get my hands on him."

Maribelle's rapid-fire remarks left no room for London to speak. She really shouldn't sleep with Harrison Crosby, but any argument about what a bad idea it was would fall on deaf ears.

"Need I remind you that you're engaged? You better tone down your fan-girling," London warned. "Beau might not appreciate you heaping praise on another man."

"Don't you worry. My Beau knows while my eyes might wander my heart never will."

It was such a sweet and solemn declaration that London felt a flare of envy. Had she ever embraced that level of dedication to Linc? Not that she'd needed to. Once she'd settled on him as her future mate, she'd never looked at anyone else. And until the very end, she'd thought Linc felt the same. Her trust in him had never wavered despite all the women she knew must be throwing themselves at him while he was out of town during baseball season. She'd never imagined her competition would be someone so unassuming and close to home.

"You're lucky to have each other," London said and meant it.

"You'll find someone," Maribelle returned, her tone low and fierce. "And he will love you and make you feel safe."

Again that word *safe*. And again, London flinched. She was a strong, capable woman who didn't need a man to make her feel safe. Yet even as her thoughts trailed over this mantra, a tiny part of her clenched in hungry longing. What would it be like to be taken care of? Not physically or financially, but emotionally supported. To be part of a devoted team like Maribelle and Beau.

It was something she hadn't known growing up. Her parents had burdened her with huge—if differing— expectations. Her father was an autocratic businessman who'd impressed upon her that absolute success was the only option. London had spent her childhood living in terror that she would be criticized for not achieving high enough marks. She'd undertaken a rigorous class schedule, participated in student government, women's soccer and debate club, and couldn't remember a time during her high school and college years when she wasn't worn out or anxiety ridden.

Nor was her mother any less demanding. If her father expected her to succeed professionally, her mother had her sights set on London's social achievements. To that end, there had been hours of volunteer work and social events her mother dragged her to. Becoming engaged to Linc had been a triumph. But even then it grew obvious that no matter how much London did, it was never enough.

"I just texted Beau," Maribelle said. "He suggests we fly up on Saturday and back on Sunday. So we can see the practice rounds. Will that work for you? Usually you have parties on Saturday night, don't you?"

As easy as it would be to use work as an excuse, she heard the excitement in her friend's voice and sighed in surrender. "All we have is a small anniversary party and Annette is handling that." To London's surprise, she realized she was looking forward to getting out of town. She'd been working like a madwoman since Linc had ended their engagement. Keeping busy was the best way to avoid dwelling on her failed relationship. "And since Beau is flying us up, I'll take care of the hotel rooms."

"We should go shopping for something to wear. In fact, we should go shopping right now."

London imagined her friend grabbing her purse and heading for her car. "What's the hurry?"

"I need to make sure you wear something on your date tonight that doesn't scream *I'm not interested in getting laid.*"

"I'm not," London protested.

"Have you been with anyone since Linc?"

London winced. "You know I haven't."

"You need a rebound relationship. I think Harrison Crosby would be perfect."

That Maribelle had echoed what London herself had been thinking less than an hour earlier didn't surprise her. The two women had been friends so long they sometimes finished each other's sentences.

"Why do you say that?" London asked.

"Because he's the furthest thing from someone you'd ever settle down with, so that makes him a good bet for a casual fling."

London was warming to the idea of a quick, steamy interlude with the sexy race-car driver. Still, she'd never slept with anyone she didn't have feelings for. Yet with what she, Everly and Zoe were up to, maybe the fact that London wasn't going to fall for the guy was a plus.

"You might be right."

Maybe it would be okay to give sexual chemistry and a casual relationship a quick spin. They were both adults. What harm could it do?

Three

Harrison arrived at The Front Porch ten minutes early and parked himself at the bar in easy range of the entrance to wait for London's arrival. Since leaving her office that morning, he'd been half expecting she'd call to cancel. With each hour that passed, he'd grown increasingly confident that she wasn't going to fight their mutual attraction. Yet now, as he counted down the minutes until she walked in, he found his stomach tying itself into anxious knots.

Her effect on him should've sent him running in the opposite direction. Already he suspected that they were at odds on several fundamental issues. For one thing, she wasn't his type and it was pretty clear he wasn't hers. She was elegant and aloof. Completely the opposite of the fun-loving ladies who hung out at the track, enjoyed drinking beer and weren't afraid to get a little dirty.

He imagined she'd be bossy as hell in a relationship. Tonight was a good example. She'd chosen the time and place, taking control, making it clear if he wanted to play, it would be by her rules. Harrison smirked. She could make all the rules she wanted. He'd bend every one.

The restaurant's front door opened, and before Harrison had fully focused on the woman on the threshold, his heart gave a hard jerk. For someone accustomed to facing near collisions at ridiculous speeds and regularly operating at high levels of stress for long periods of time without faltering, Harrison wasn't sure what to make of the jolt London's arrival had given him.

For the space of several irregular breaths as her gaze swept the restaurant in search of him, Harrison had the opportunity to take her in. She'd changed her clothes since their earlier meeting and looked stunning in a navy dress with a broad neckline that bared her delicate shoulders and the hollows above her collarbones. The material hugged her upper body, highlighting the curves of her breasts, before flaring into a full skirt that stopped at her knees. The dark color contrasted with the creamy tones of her pale skin and highlighted her blue eyes. She'd pulled her hair back into a loose knot at the base of her neck and left long strands of gold waves to frame her face. Her only jewelry was a pair of simple pearl earrings.

When she spotted him, her uncertain smile hit Harrison like lightning. His nerves buzzed in the aftermath as he made his way through the crowded bar toward her.

"You look gorgeous," he murmured, cupping his fingers around her bare arm and leaning down to graze a kiss across her cheek.

Her body tensed at his familiarity, but her smile remained in place as he stepped back and looked down at her.

"Thank you," she said, her voice neither breathless nor coy. She took in his jeans, light blue shirt and oatmeal colored blazer. "You look quite dapper," she said, reaching out to tug at the navy pocket square in his breast pocket.

"I'm glad you approve," he said and meant it. "And I'm glad you were able to join me for dinner tonight."

"You were kind to invite me."

Niceties concluded, Harrison set his hand on her back and guided her toward the hostess. They were led to a table by the front windows overlooking King Street.

"Do you come here a lot?" Harrison asked after they were seated. He scanned the menu, which specialized in farm-to-table fare, and settled on the scallops with smoked yogurt, beets and pistachio.

"Actually, I've never been, but it's one of Maribelle and Beau's favorite places. They had their first date here and…it's where he proposed." Her eyes widened as if she realized what she'd implied. "They're always going on and on about how good the food is. That's why I picked it."

"Can't wait to see if they're right."

"So, you've never been here before?"

Harrison shook his head. "I don't get out much."

"I find that hard to believe."

"It's true. I'm on the road so much of the year that when I do get home, I like to hole up and recharge."

"You do?"

"Most of my time and attention is focused on cars and racing. Analyzing my competition, studying the track, figuring out how I can improve."

"I did a little research on you and learned you're a big deal in racing." Bright spots of color appeared in her cheeks as he raised his eyebrows at her confession. "Lots of appearances and events."

"All to promote Crosby Motorsports. I'm actually an introvert." He could tell she wasn't buying it.

"You can't possibly be. You're a fan favorite with a huge following."

"Don't get me wrong, I do my share of press events and meeting fans, but it isn't what I enjoy. I'd much rather be tinkering with a car or hanging out with a few of my friends."

She made a face. "I figured you would be out in the public, soaking up the accolades, enjoying your stardom."

Her thorny tone made him frown. "You seem to have a very jaded view of me. Why is that?"

"It's not you." She moved her wineglass around in circles on the white tablecloth and seemed engrossed in the light refracted by the liquid. "I guess it's what you do. I've spent a lot of time around sports stars and most of them love being celebrities. The adoring fans. The special attention they get wherever they go. It makes them act…entitled."

Obviously her attitude had been formed during her relationship with Lincoln Thurston. As a professional baseball player, no doubt Thurston had enjoyed his share of the limelight. Harrison needed to convince her he and her ex-fiancé weren't cut from the same cloth.

"Not all of them," Harrison insisted.

"Most of them."

"Was Linc that way?" He'd asked, even knowing that it was risky to probe for details about what might be painful for her.

"I don't want to talk about him." London's brittle tone was a warning to Harrison that he should tread carefully.

Still, he needed to know where her head was at. "Because you're still not over the breakup?"

How could she be? He'd done his own bit of research on her and discovered only a few months had passed since their two-year engagement ended.

"I am over it." The bits of gold floating in London's blue eyes flashed.

"Are you over him?"

She exhaled in exasperation. "We were together for three years."

"So that's a no?"

London's expression hardened into a look that Harrison interpreted as *back off*. That wasn't going to stop him. This woman was worth fighting for.

"I can't imagine what having him break your engagement must have been like for you, but I am happy to listen if you want to dump on the guy." He paused and then grinned. "Or the male gender as a whole."

From her frown, he could see his offer had confused her.

"Why?"

He shrugged. "Because I think too many men suck in the way they treat women."

"And you don't?" Her earlier tension faded into skepticism.

"I'm sure you can find plenty of women who would complain about me."

One corner of her lips twitched. "So what, then, makes you so different from all the other men out there?"

"Maybe nothing. Or maybe it's the case that I don't take advantage of people because I can. I'm not an entitled jerk like my brother can be all too often." Harrison brought up Tristan to see how London reacted. She'd shown far too much interest in him at the party and Harrison wanted to understand why. "Tristan treats women like they're his personal playground."

"But until recently he's been married. Are you insinuating he wasn't faithful?" London's interest intensified when Harrison shook his head. "I've never understood why men bother being in a relationship if they intend to cheat."

Harrison recalled what his uncle Bennett had told him about Linc Thurston's infidelity. London had every right to be skittish when it came to trusting any guy she perceived as having the same sort of fame and fortune as her ex-fiancé.

"It's a social norm."

London looked positively dumbstruck. "Is that what you think?"

"It's true, isn't it?" Harrison countered.

"What about love?"

"Not everyone believes in love. I don't think my brother does. Tristan chose to marry a very beautiful, very young, woman who was passive and pliable. For eight years she satisfied his need for a decorative and docile companion." Harrison recalled how Zoe's spirit dimmed with each wedding anniversary. "Her only failure was in her inability to make my brother happy."

"Why was that her responsibility?" London asked in surprise. "Isn't marriage a partnership where you support each other?"

"Mine will be." Harrison waited a beat to see how she absorbed that before continuing, "I think Zoe's dissatisfaction with her role grew too strong to be contained. One thing about Tristan—he likes having his way and becomes a bear if events run counter to his preferences. I imagine him perceiving Zoe's discontent as nothing he'd done wrong, but a failing on her part."

London absorbed his assessment for several seconds before asking, "How close are you with his ex-wife?"

"I like Zoe. She's quiet and subdued, but once you get to know her you see that she has a warm heart and a wry sense of humor." He could go on extolling her virtues but decided to keep to his original purpose, which was to make sure London understood that Tristan wasn't a good guy. "She deserved better than my brother."

"I hope she appreciated having you as her champion."

"I don't know about that. If I'd been a better friend, I would've steered her away from marrying Tristan."

"You might not have been able to do that. Sometimes we have to make our own mistakes. It's the only way we learn."

"Maybe, but some mistakes carry harsher consequences than others."

London sat back and let her hands slide into her lap. She regarded him steadily with her keen blue eyes. "You aren't what I expected."

"I hope that's a good thing."

"The jury is still out," she said, an enigmatic smile kicking up the corners of her lips. "So, Mr. Introvert, what is it you enjoy besides cars and racing?"

"The usual guy stuff. Outdoor sports. Spending time with my friends. How about you? What do you do when you're not working?"

She laughed. "Sleep and eat. Sometimes I get a massage or facial. I have a hard time unwinding."

"Sounds like we're both on the go a lot."

"Like a shark. Swim or die."

The phone in her purse chimed. She'd set the clutch on the table beside her plate and now made a face at it. "Sorry." The tone repeated.

"Do you need to get that?"

"No." She heaved a sigh. "I already know what it's about."

"That's impressive," he teased and was rewarded with a grimace.

"About this weekend..."

Something in her tone made him grin. "You've decided to accept my invitation to watch me race in Richmond."

"I spoke with Maribelle," she replied. "Both she and her fiancé are excited about your offer."

Her carefully worded statement left room for interpretation. "What about you?"

"I'm not sure what I'm getting into, so I'm reserving judgment."

"I guess that's something," he murmured, convinced he would win her over.

"We're flying up Saturday morning," she continued, ignoring his dry remark. "And Beau was wondering if you'd be able to get us into the pit. At least I think that's what he wanted to know."

"Absolutely."

She'd been seated facing the restaurant's entrance and suddenly her eyes went wide in surprise. Harrison drew a breath to ask what was wrong when she shifted her attention back to him and smiled brightly.

"You know..." she began, picking up her purse. "Maybe I should double-check the text to make sure nothing is amiss." She gave a nervous half laugh. "The pitfall of being the boss is that I'm always on call. Excuse me, won't you?"

And before Harrison could say anything, she'd fled the table, leaving him staring over his shoulder after her.

Everly Briggs strode along King Street, paying little attention to the restaurants, stores and bars clustered along the popular thoroughfare. Her entire focus was on the tall man she was following.

Linc Thurston appeared unaware of the stir he caused as he passed. Usually the professional baseball player paused to chat with fans he encountered, but tonight he seemed intent on reaching his destination.

Since Everly, London and Zoe had met at the Beautiful Women Taking Charge event, Everly had been actively pursuing whatever angle she could to take down Linc. From digging into all available gossip, Everly had gotten wind that the reason he'd broken off his engagement to London was that he'd started cheating on her with his housekeeper.

Once she'd determined that they weren't just involved in a fling, but a full-blown, secret relationship, she determined this would be the best way to get revenge on him. At the moment she had plans in the works to expose the woman's lies and sabotage her credibility. Linc would learn what it meant to be betrayed by someone he loved.

Of course, her plans would completely fall apart if she was wrong about the strength of his feelings for Claire Robbins, so Everly was doing a little spying to see if his cheating was a onetime event or if the man was a typical representation of his gender.

She was so caught up in her thoughts that Everly hadn't noticed Linc had stopped walking until she drew within arm's length. Jerking to a halt would be too obvious, so Everly was forced to sail on past. She did take note of what had captured his interest, however, and spotted London occupying a table beside the large window of The Front Porch. She was obviously having dinner with Harrison Crosby and the couple was engaged in some pretty serious flirting.

What the hell was London doing? She was supposed to be taking down Tristan Crosby, not dating his brother.

Everly's irritation spiked as she reached the end of the block. By the time she turned the corner, she'd pulled out her phone. Pausing, she typed a text and sent it. Although the three women had agreed not to communicate to avoid their plotting being discovered, Everly simply had to confront London.

We need to meet—E

She tapped her foot as she waited for a response. Meanwhile she kept her gaze on King Street, expecting Linc to pass by at any second. She'd intended to continue her surveillance and it annoyed her that London's behavior was forcing her to detour. When her phone didn't immediately chime with an answer from London, Everly rapidly typed a second message.

I saw you having dinner tonight. What r u doing?

When London still didn't answer, Everly knew she had no choice but to push the issue.

Linc had passed by while Everly had been typing her second text. Instead of following him, she doubled back to the restaurant. London sat facing the entrance and Everly made sure the woman noticed her enter. The two made brief eye contact before Everly headed toward the back, where the restrooms were located.

She entered the ladies' room and was relieved to find the stalls empty. She approached the sinks and pulled her lipstick out. Fury made her hands shake. While she was here dealing with London, Linc was getting away.

By the time London pushed through the door, Everly was more than ready to let her have it.

"Why are you having dinner with Harrison Crosby?" she snarled, barely restraining the urge to shout in displeasure. "You're supposed to be going after Tristan."

"What are you doing here?" London countered, pitching her voice barely above a whisper. "We agreed the way this works is to not have any contact with each other. We can't be seen together."

"I came to find out why you're going after the wrong brother," Everly said, ignoring London's objections.

London crossed her arms over her chest and glared back. "Did it ever occur to you that Harrison might be the best way for me to get close to Tristan?"

Everly let loose a disparaging noise. How could London possibly think she was buying that? It was obvious what was going on.

"It's more likely that you find him attractive and plan on sleeping with him." Based on the way London refused to meet Everly's gaze, she'd hit it square on the head. "Do you have any idea how badly that could backfire?"

"Look," London said, showing no sign of being convinced that her actions were flawed. "It's none of your business how I handle my end of the bargain. You and I meeting like this could become a problem if anyone sees us together and it's discovered that you were behind whatever happens with Linc."

"Give me some credit," Everly snapped. "No one's

ever going to find out I was the one behind what happens to him."

"Regardless. We agreed this only works if we don't have any contact with each other. So leave me alone."

Before Everly could say another word, London flung open the bathroom door and exited.

For several long minutes Everly fumed. This situation with London and Harrison Crosby was a problem. Now she had to keep her eye on her own revenge scenario and make sure London stayed focused on their plan. And if London couldn't do the job, then Everly would show her what happened when you turned your back on your friends.

Four

With her heart pumping hard against her ribs, London smoothed her palms along her dress's full skirt and slowly wound her way back to Harrison. Everly's texts and subsequent appearance in the restaurant had been disturbing. What they were doing was dangerous enough. If they were caught in some sort of conspiracy, it could ruin all their lives.

Nor could she ignore the question front and center in her thoughts. Was Everly following her? The possibility made her skin prickle. How else could the other woman have known that London was having dinner with Harrison? And what sort of insanity had prompted Everly to confront London in public like this where anyone could have seen them? Had Everly contacted Zoe, as well? London was tempted to reach out to the third member of their scheme, but that was exactly what she'd railed at Everly for doing.

Anxiety danced along her nerve endings as she slid into her seat opposite Harrison. London suspected her distress was reflected in her expression because after a quick survey of her face, he frowned.

"Is everything okay?"

"Fine." London forced a reassuring smile. "I just received a bit of bad news about an event I was going to organize." The lie came too easily, sparking concern over the person she was becoming. "The client had been on the fence about what they wanted to do and decided to cancel."

"You seem rattled. It must've been a big client."

"Not huge, but all my clients are equally important and I'm disappointed that this didn't work out." Even though London wasn't lying, the fact that she was deceiving Harrison left a bad taste in her mouth.

"Maybe they'll change their mind." His winning smile gave her heart a different reason to pound. "I'll bet you can be quite persuasive."

His attempt to make her feel better through flattery was turning her insides to mush and soothing away her earlier distress. She caught herself smiling at him in gratitude as pleasure washed over her. The man had a knack for getting under her skin.

"If by 'persuasive' you mean bossy," London said, recognizing that she had a tendency to stab directly into the heart of something rather than nibble away at the edges, "then I agree. I come on a little too strong sometimes."

"You want to get things done," Harrison said, nodding. "I get it. Winning is everything."

It struck London that maybe they had more in common than she'd initially thought. They shared a love of competition and a matching determination to get across the finish line. Maybe his way of doing things meant he slid behind the wheel of a car and drove at reckless and adrenaline-inducing speeds, making impulsive decisions in the moment, while she tended to be more methodical and deliberate in her approach.

"I don't exactly think of it as winning," London responded. "More like a job well done."

"Nothing wrong with that."

London toyed with her earring as she asked, "Do you win a lot?"

"I've had my share of successes over the years. Generally, I finish in the top ten drivers about two-thirds of the time. Except for the first couple years when I was still learning and a couple of seasons when injury kept me off the track."

"Is that good?" she asked, noting his amusement and figuring she'd just displayed total ignorance of what he did.

"It's a decent statistic."

"So winning isn't important?"

"Of course it's important, but with thirty-six races a year, it's impossible to be on top all the time. If I win four to six times in a season, that's good enough to put me in the top three for the year as long as my stats are solid."

As an event planner, London was accustomed to

dealing with a lot of numbers. It was how she kept her clients happy while maximizing their budget and remaining profitable. She was interested in trying to understand the way driver standings were determined.

"How many other drivers are there?"

"Almost sixty."

"What was your worst year?"

"The year I started—2004. I finished fifty-eighth."

"How old were you?"

"Nineteen." Harrison's lips twisted in self-deprecating humor. "And I thought I knew everything there was to know."

London considered what she'd been like at nineteen and couldn't relate. She'd been a freshman in college, away from her parents for the first time and struggling to figure out who she was.

"And now?" she prompted.

"Still learning," he said. "Always improving."

"Those seem like good words to live by," she said.

His blend of confidence and humility was endearing. London softened still more toward him even as she marveled at his gamesmanship.

The waitress approached to check on their meal and London watched the man across from her charm the woman with his friendliness. The contrast between the two brothers struck her again. During her brief introduction to Tristan, the way the man had looked her over had made London feel like running home and taking a shower.

"Did you leave any room for dessert?" the waitress asked.

Harrison glanced her way and London shook her head. "But don't let me stop you from ordering something."

"I hate to eat alone." And once the waitress had left with their plates, Harrison finished, "Besides, I'd much rather grab an ice cream cone at Swenson's."

"I haven't been there in years," London said, remembering what a rare treat it had been when her father had taken her there.

"Then it's time to go, don't you think?" He didn't wait for her answer before asking, "What is your favorite flavor? Please don't say vanilla."

"I don't know." She was struck by rising delight at the thought of enjoying such a simple, satisfying treat with Harrison. "Maybe strawberry."

"A few months ago they introduced a strawberry, honey balsamic, with black pepper ice cream. It's really good."

"You know quite a bit about the place." London's mouth watered as she imagined all those delicious flavors harmonizing on her taste buds. "Do you take all your dates there?" She didn't mean the question to sound so flippant and flushed beneath his keen regard.

"You'd be the first."

"That was rude of me. I'm sorry."

"Are you skeptical of all men?" he asked. "Or is it just me?"

She took a second to consider his question before answering. "Not all men and not you. It's just that since Linc and I..." She wished she hadn't brought up her ex-fiancé's name again. "The breakup has left me feeling exposed and I lash out at unexpected moments. I'm sorry."

"He really hurt you."

"Yes and no." She really didn't want to talk about Linc over a first-date dinner with Harrison, but maybe it would be good to clear the air. "All my life I've achieved whatever I set my mind to. Except for one thing. Social acceptance in certain circles. In Charleston it's impossible to become an insider. You have to be born into it. When Linc and I got engaged, it opened doors I'd spent my life knocking on."

London sighed as she finished her explanation. She wanted Harrison to understand what had driven her. His own family was self-made, parlaying hard work into a booming automotive empire. Would he view her hunger to belong to a group of "insiders" as petty and shallow?

"Growing up, I attended the right schools," she continued, thinking back to the private all-girl high school she'd attended and the friends she'd made there. Friends who'd gone on to attend debutante classes and formal teas and to participate in the father/daughter skeet shoot. "But I was always on the outside looking in."

"And that bothered you a lot."

Despite his neutral tone, her defensiveness flared. "Shouldn't it?"

"Why did you think you needed the validation? In my opinion, you already have it all."

Delight set all her nerve endings alight and suddenly a lifetime of exclusion became less hurtful. "That's kind of you to say, but it never seemed enough." Seeing the questions in Harrison's raised eyebrows, London explained further. "My mother is constantly harping on how frustrating it is for her that no matter how much money she donates or how lavish her dinner parties are, she can't ever gain acceptance."

"So maybe it's your mother's issue and not yours."

If only it was that simple.

"She's pretty determined." London could've said more about her mother's unrelenting pressure on her to marry well, but decided further explanations would only put her family's flaws on display.

"It seems like a lot of pressure."

London shrugged. "I'm no stranger to that. After all, heat and extreme pressure turns coal into diamonds," she said, parroting her mother's favorite quote.

"That's not actually a scientific fact," Harrison replied.

"Fine," she grumbled. "But diamonds need heat and pressure to form."

His lips curved in a bone-melting smile. "True."

The exchange highlighted how easily Harrison could blow past her defenses and signaled to London that she might be mistaken about which Crosby brother presented the most danger to her.

Everly's words came back to London. Maybe the other woman's concerns weren't out of line. Did she have what it took to keep up her end of the bargain when already she was thinking of Harrison in terms of getting to know him better rather than someone she could use?

Fifteen minutes later Harrison opened the restaurant's front door, and as soon as they reached the sidewalk, he took her hand and threaded it through his arm. Already a warm glow filled her as a result of the wine she'd consumed and Harrison's stimulating company. Being tucked close against his body increased the heat beneath her skin and she inhaled the cool fresh air, hoping it would clear her head.

"Thinking about ice cream?" he asked, breaking into her thoughts. They'd reached the corner, and instead of continuing on to Swenson's, he pulled her onto the quieter thoroughfare. "Because I'm not."

"No?" she countered, trembling as he backed her up against the building's brick wall and leaned his forearm beside her head.

His gaze searched her features before settling on her lips. "The only dessert I want is a taste of your sweet lips."

If any other man had delivered that line, she would've had a cynical retort, but something about Harrison told her that he meant every word. Her muscles lost strength, making her glad for the wall at her back. She wasn't sure what to do with her hands. His hard body called to her, but letting her palms roam over his chiseled physique—while tempting—was a little too familiar for their first… dinner…date?

"Okay."

"Okay?" he echoed, his soft, firm lips grazing across hers with deliberate intent.

"Yes." She breathed the word and it came out sounding almost like a plea.

"Are you sure it's not too forward of me?"

He seemed determined to tantalize and torment her with what could be. The suggestion of a kiss did exactly what it was supposed to. It frustrated her and provoked curiosity at the same time. She reached up and tunneled her fingers into his hair.

"Kiss me like you want to," she urged, conflicting notes of desperation and command in her tone as he trailed his lips across her cheek.

"If I do that, we might get arrested." His husky laugh puffed against her skin, making her shiver.

Disturbed by the acute longing he aroused, London laid her palm against his chest. His rapid heartbeat caught her attention and bolstered her confidence. The chemistry she felt wasn't one-sided but sparkled between them, ripe with promise and potential.

"I don't know what to do with you," she murmured, trembling as his hand slipped around her waist and into the small of her back, drawing her tight against his hard body.

"Funny," he said. "I know exactly what to do with you." His fingers coasted over the curve of her butt and he punctuated his claim with a quick squeeze before setting her free. "You are temptation in high heels."

The heavy beat of desire pulsing between her thighs made it hard for London to utter her next words. "I think I'd better go home."

"I'll walk you to your car."

To her dismay, his words disappointed her. As they made their way to the parking lot where she'd left her car, she mulled several questions. How had she hoped the evening might end? That he would press her to extend their time together? Suggest that she come home with him?

He'd demonstrated that he was attracted to her…hadn't he? Wasn't that what he'd meant by his temptation-in-high-heels remark? He spoke as if he wanted her, but his actions hadn't crossed any boundaries she'd set for first-date behavior. His kisses hadn't been designed to blow past her defenses and set her afire. She had no doubt that would happen. The brief contact with him had demonstrated her body was dry kindling and his lips the spark that would set her alight.

"Are you okay?" he asked, breaking into her thoughts.

"Fine." Yet she was anything but. What if there was something wrong with her? Something that caused men to lose interest in sex. Could it be that she was the sort of woman who turned men off? Harrison had barely kissed her. Maybe he'd been uninterested in taking things any further.

London's skin prickled as she pondered her relationship with Linc. For months now she'd been plagued by the worry that the reason he'd broken off their engagement was her lack of desirability. Sure, sex between them had been good. Linc was a fantastic lover and she'd never gone unsatisfied. But there hadn't ever been the sort of rip-your-clothes-off passion Maribelle so often talked about having with Beau. In fact, London had grown surly with her best friend several times after Maribelle had shared stories about her and her fiancé.

"Remember I told you I was an introvert?"

"Yes."

"Aside from the negative impression we can give about being shy, aloof or stuck-up, we have a lot of really positive characteristics. One of those being our ability to take in a lot of information and process it."

Unsure what he was getting at, London asked, "What sort of information?"

"When I'm in the middle of a race, it can be tiny nuances about how other cars are moving that telegraph what their drivers are thinking. I'm also pretty good at reading micro-expressions. I can tell by tiny muscle shifts what someone might be feeling."

"You think you know what I'm feeling?" She disliked being like a bug under a microscope.

"I can tell you're not happy."

Rather than agree or disagree, she raised one eyebrow and stared at him.

"You can give me that face all day, but I'm not the one you're upset with."

"What makes you think I'm upset at anyone?"

"Not anyone. Yourself."

That he had read her so easily should've rattled London, but there was no judgment in his manner. "And I suppose you know why?"

"I could guess, but I'd rather wait until you're ready to tell me."

He couldn't have said anything better, and all at once London wanted to cry. She prided herself on her strength and resilience. That Harrison had whipped up her hormones, roused her insecurities and nearly reduced her to tears demonstrated just how dangerous he could be.

"What if I never do?"

To her shock, he wrapped her in a fierce, platonic hug that left her body tingling and her nerves raw.

"Everyone needs someone to talk to, London," he whispered and then let her go. Before she could untie her tongue, he continued, "I'll call you later this week with the details about Saturday. I'm looking forward to having you and your friends at the race."

London used the distraction of sliding behind the wheel to grab at her flailing control and reined in her wayward emotions. "Is there anything I should know beforehand?"

"We're looking at sunshine and midsixties for race day, so dress accordingly."

"Okay." London had no idea what to wear to a racetrack, but no doubt Maribelle would have plenty of ideas. "I'll see you Saturday."

"See you Saturday." With a wink, Harrison stepped back so she could close the car door.

"Harrison!" Jack Crosby's sharp tone brought his nephew back to the present. "What is going on with you? All week you've been distracted."

His uncle wasn't wrong.

It was early Saturday afternoon. The qualifying races had run that morning, and instead of revisiting his performance on the Richmond track, a certain blonde kept popping up in his thoughts, disrupting his ability to stay on task.

His usual hyper focus on the days leading up to a race had been compromised while he'd wasted energy regretting that he'd pulled back instead of making a definite move on her like she seemed to expect.

Yet her conflict had been plain. She'd made it clear

that he wasn't the sort of man she saw herself with, but their undeniable chemistry tempted her. Based on how she'd begged him to kiss her, no doubt he'd gotten beneath her skin. Which was exactly why he'd retreated instead of wearing down her defenses. The woman was too quick to lay down the law. She had definite boundaries and ideas how courtship was supposed to transpire. He needed to set the foundation for new ground rules.

"I guess I've been a little off."

"A little?" His uncle crossed his arms over his chest. "I've never seen you like this."

"I'm sure it's not that bad."

"Since the day you showed up at Crosby Motorsports and declared that you were going to be our top driver one day, you've been the most focused member of the team. And that's saying something considering all the talent we've assembled. But not this week."

Harrison spied a trio headed their way along the alley between the garages and felt his lips curve into a giant grin. He'd recognized Maribelle right off. The lean, well-dressed man matching her brisk pace had to be her fiancé. And the leggy blonde trailing them looked like a fish out of water as her gaze swung this way and that, taking in the loud cars and mechanics that buzzed around the vehicles.

"Excuse me a second," he said to his uncle before stepping forward to meet the visitors.

"Welcome to Richmond," he said as he drew near enough to shake hands. "Hello, Maribelle. And you must be her fiancé, Beau. I'm Harrison Crosby."

"Beau Shelton." The man clasped hands with Harrison. "No need to introduce yourself. We're big fans." Beau tipped his head to indicate Maribelle and she nodded vigorously. "We appreciate this chance to get a glimpse behind the scenes."

"I'm glad you came," Harrison said, forcing himself to be patient when all he wanted was to push past the couple and snatch London into his arms.

Maribelle winked at him. "Thanks for the invite."

Harrison approved of her sassy demeanor, even as he noted once again how her outgoing personality differed from her friend's reserve. Given how close the two women seemed to be, Harrison hoped it boded well for his own chances with London. Obviously she liked— and definitely needed—someone in her life who encouraged her to have fun once in a while.

"Hi," he murmured to London after the couple stepped to one side to allow him access to their friend. He ignored her tentativeness and leaned down to brush his lips over her cheek. "I'm really happy you're here."

London peered at him from beneath her lashes. "You were kind to invite us."

"You look amazing."

She'd chosen dark blue skinny jeans with strategic tears that gave them a trendy appearance, an oversize fuzzy white sweater and a camel-toned moto jacket that matched the suede pumps on her tiny feet. She looked as if she'd worked hard to dress down, but hadn't succeeded in achieving her friend's casual weekend style. His fingers itched to slide into the low knot she'd fastened her hair into and shake the pins loose. She needed someone like him to mess up her perfect appearance.

"I like your suit." Her deliberate scan of his body heated his blood. "It's very colorful."

Fighting the urge to find a quiet corner where he could kiss that sardonic grin off her beautiful lips, Harrison stuck to polite conversation.

"How was the flight down?"

"It was a little more eventful than usual." Her blue eyes shifted past him and settled on her friends. "Beau is teaching Maribelle how to fly and today she did both the takeoff and landing."

"It was fine," Maribelle piped up. "Just a little windier than I was used to during the landing. I did a perfectly acceptable job, didn't I?" This last she directed to her fiancé, who nodded.

His heart was in his eyes as he grinned down at her. "You did great."

Envy twisted in Harrison's chest at the couple's obvious connection. The emotion caught him off guard. Over the last decade he'd watched most of his team and fellow drivers fall in love and get married. Many had even started families. Not once had he wanted to trade places. But since meeting London, he was starting to notice a pronounced dissatisfaction with his personal life.

"That's my car in the third garage stall on the left, if you want to check it out."

"I've never seen a race car up close before," Maribelle said, tugging at Beau's hand to get him going. "I have a hundred questions."

Harrison let London's friends walk ahead of them. The urge to touch her couldn't be denied, so he bumped the back of his hand against hers to see how she'd react. She shot him a questioning glance even as she twisted her wrist so that her palm met his. As his fingers closed around hers, a lazy grin slid over his lips.

"This is…really something." Her choice of words left him with no idea how she felt, but her gaze darted around as if she half expected to be run over any second. "There's a lot of activity."

Up and down the length of the garage, the crews swarmed their cars, making last-minute tweaks before the final practice of the day. Today was a little less chaotic for Harrison than race day and he was delighted to be able to give London and her friends a tour.

"If you think this is hectic, wait until tomorrow. Things really kick into high gear then."

"So, you look like you're dressed to get behind the wheel." She set her fingertip lightly on his chest right over his madly pumping heart. "What's going on today?"

"We had the qualifying race this morning and there are practices this afternoon."

She cocked her head like a curious bird. "You have to qualify before you can race?"

"The qualifier determines what position you start in."

"And where are you starting?"

"Tenth." He should've done better, but his excitement at seeing London again had blown a hole in his concentration. It was unexpected. No woman had thrown him off his game before.

"Is that good?"

Based on the tongue-lashing delivered by his uncle, not so much.

"In a pack of forty," Harrison said with an offhanded shrug. "It's okay."

Nor was it his worst start all year. A month ago his car had failed the inspection before the qualifying race because of a piece of tape on his spoiler and he'd ended up starting in thirty-sixth position.

"So I'll get to see you drive this afternoon?"

"We have a fifty-minute practice happening at three." He took her hand in his and drew her forward. "Come meet my team and check out the car."

After introducing London and her friends to his uncle and giving them a quick tour of the garage, Harrison directed Beau and Maribelle to a spot where they could watch the practice laps. Before letting London get away, he caught her hand and stopped while they were twenty feet from the stall where his car sat.

"You know, I've been thinking about you all week," he confessed, mesmerized by the bright gold shards floating in her blue eyes.

"I've been thinking about you, too." And then, as if she'd given too much away, she finished with, "We have several venues to look at on Monday and I have lots of ideas to run past you for the decor."

He ignored her attempt to turn the conversation to business and leaned close. "I've been regretting that I didn't take you up on your offer."

Her tone was husky as she asked, "What offer was that?"

He pinched a fold of her suede jacket between his

fingers and tugged her a half step toward him until their thighs brushed. At the glancing contact, she bit down on her lower lip.

"When you told me to kiss you any way I want."

"That was in the heat of the moment," she said, her voice soft and a trifle breathless. "I don't know what I was thinking."

"I was kinda hoping you weren't thinking at all."

"I guess I wasn't." She gave him a wry smile. "Because if I had been, I probably wouldn't have gone out with you in the first place." Her lighthearted tone took the punch out of her words.

"I'm gonna guess you think too much."

"I'm gonna guess you do, too," she said.

"Most of the time, but not when I'm around you. Then all I do is feel." Harrison cupped her face and sent his thumb skimming across her lower lip. Her eyes widened in surprise. "In fact, my uncle is annoyed with me because it's been hard for me to stay focused."

The temptation to dip his head and kiss her in full view of her friends, his uncle and the racing team nearly overcame him until she gently pulled his hand away and gave it a brief squeeze.

"You're quite the flirt," she said.

"I'm not flirting. I'm speaking one-hundred-percent unvarnished truth." He spread his fingers and entwined them with hers. "Will you have dinner with me tonight?"

"All of us?" she quizzed, glancing after her departing friends.

"Of course. You're my guests." He liked that she looked ever so briefly disappointed. Had she hoped to have dinner alone with him? "I have a press event at six. How about if I pick you up at eight?"

She glanced at the couple ahead of them. "That should be fine."

"Terrific." His gaze drifted to her soft lips. "A kiss for luck?"

"I thought it was just a practice," she retorted, arching one eyebrow. "Why do you need luck?"

"It's always dangerous when you get onto the track," he said, his voice pitched to a persuasive tone as he tugged her to him. "A thousand different things could go wrong."

"Well, I wouldn't want to be responsible for anything like that." Reaching up, she deposited a light kiss on his cheek.

It wasn't exactly what he'd had in mind, but Harrison's temperature skyrocketed in response to the light press of her breasts against his chest. He curved his fingers over the swell of her hip just below the indent of her waist, keeping her near for a heart-stopping second.

Too soon she was stepping back, the color in her cheeks high. Harrison wondered if his face was equally flushed because he appreciated the cool breeze blowing through the alley between the garages.

"Good luck, Harrison," London told him before turning to follow her friends. "Don't let that kiss go to waste."

With a rueful shake of his head, Harrison returned to the garage and wasn't surprised to find several of his pit crew ready to razz him over his obvious infatuation with London.

"She's obviously a great gal," Jack Crosby remarked

flatly. "Now, can you please stop mooning over her and focus on the next fifty minutes?"

Harrison smirked at his uncle. "Jack, if you weren't so in love with your wife of forty years, I might think you were jealous."

Five

Anxiety had settled in by the time the clock on the nightstand in her hotel room hit seven fifty. London stared at her reflection, hemming and hawing over the third outfit she'd tried on.

She'd overdressed for today's visit to the racetrack. What might have suited a shopping trip in downtown Charleston had stood out like a sore thumb at Richmond Raceway. Was tonight's navy blue sheath and beige blazer another misstep? She looked ready for a client meeting instead of a date with a sexy race-car driver. Would he show up in jeans and a T-shirt or slacks and a sweater? Should she switch to the black skinny pants and white blouse she'd packed? London was on her way to the closet when a knock sounded on her door.

For a second her heart threatened to explode from her

chest until she remembered that she'd agreed to meet Harrison in the lobby. He didn't have her room number, so there was no way he could be the one knocking on her door. She went to answer and spied Beau standing in the hallway. His eyebrows went up when he glimpsed her.

"You're wearing that to dinner?"

London had grown fond of Beau over the last three years, but having him critique her wardrobe choices was too much. She crossed her arms over her chest and glared at him.

"I am." Why did everyone find it necessary to criticize her appearance? "What's wrong with it?" She meant to sound hostile and defensive but the question came out sounding concerned.

"It's a dinner date," Beau pointed out, "not a business meeting."

"It's not a date," she argued, ignoring the fact that she wanted it to be. She just couldn't get attached to Harrison Crosby. Not when she was using him to get to his brother. "We're just four people having dinner."

"About that..." Beau began, his gaze sliding in the direction of the hotel room he was sharing with his fiancée. "Maribelle isn't feeling well, so we're going to stay in tonight and order room service."

London knew immediately that her friend was completely fine and that the engaged couple had conspired to set London up to have dinner alone with Harrison. Panic set in.

"But it's too late for me to cancel," she protested. "He's supposed to be here right now."

"I'm sure it will be just fine if the two of you go by yourselves." He offered her a cheeky grin and winked. "Just wear something else. And have fun. He's a great guy if you'd just give him a chance."

"Great," she grumbled, closing the hotel room door and pondering Beau's parting words.

Harrison was showing every appearance of being a really great guy. Certainly one who deserved better than what she was doing to him. Guilt pinched her as she went to fetch her purse off the dresser. As she passed the closet a flash of teal distracted her. She'd added the clingy fit-and-flare dress to her suitcase at the last second. The color reminded her of Harrison's eyes, a coastal blue-green she could happily drown in.

Growling at the impulses sweeping through her, London roughly stripped out of the blazer, unzipped her sensible blue dress and let it fall to the floor. A minute later she was sliding the soft jersey over her head and tugging it into place. Almost immediately London's perception of the evening before her transformed. As she turned to the dresser and the bag that held her jewelry, the full skirt ballooned and then fell to brush against her thighs, setting off a chain reaction of sensation.

The mirror above the dresser reflected a woman whose eyes glowed with anticipation. She tugged her hair free of its restraining knot and let it fall around her face before fastening on a pair of long crystal earrings that tickled her neck as she moved. A quick glance at the clock revealed she was now running late. London scooped her clothes off the floor and draped them over the bed before sliding her feet into nude pumps and snagging her purse.

It wasn't until she'd closed the hotel room door behind her and raced toward the elevator that she realized she was breathing erratically. Nor could she blame her agitation on the last-minute wardrobe change. She might as well face that she was excited to be having dinner alone with Harrison.

Since her hotel room was on the second floor, London had less than a minute to compose herself before the elevator doors opened. She stepped forward onto the smooth marble floor of the reception area.

At this hour the lobby was busy with people on their way to dinner or in search of a drink at the elegant bar. Suddenly she realized she hadn't specified a particular location in the large open area to meet Harrison. But even before her concerns could take root, he stepped into her line of sight, looking handsome, desirable and a little dangerous dressed all in black. She released a pent-up breath as he drew near.

"Hi," she said weakly.

"You look gorgeous." He leaned down and brushed her cheek with his lips.

Goose bumps broke out on her arms. "Thanks." London couldn't believe he'd reduced her to single-syllable words. "So do you." To her dismay, she felt her cheeks heat. "I mean, you look very nice."

"Thanks." He glanced past her. "Where are Maribelle and Beau?"

"She wasn't feeling well, so they're ordering room service and staying in."

He frowned. "I hope that doesn't mean they'll miss the race tomorrow."

"I think she'll make a miraculous recovery," London mused.

"Oh?" Harrison raised his eyebrows.

London cleared her throat. "She likes to play matchmaker."

"I see."

Did he? When London peered at him from beneath her lashes, she caught him observing her in turn. His look, however, was bold and openly curious.

"She thinks you're a catch."

"I mean no offense when I say that I'm not interested in what she thinks." Harrison took her hand and led her toward the lobby doors. "I want to hear your opinion."

"Do I think you're a catch?" London knew her breathless state had nothing to do with their pace. It was more about the warmth of Harrison's fingers against her skin. "Of course you are."

He glanced at her as she sailed through the open door ahead of him. "You're a little too matter-of-fact when you say that."

"How else should I be?" Despite her earlier reservations, London was having a wonderful time bantering with Harrison. "Are you hoping I'll spill the beans and divulge that I'm infatuated with you?"

"It'd be nice." But his smile indicated he wasn't serious. "Especially given how much you've been on my mind these last few days. It's getting me into trouble with my team."

He'd recaptured her hand once they'd reached the sidewalk. Was he serious? They'd only met three times and been out once. Surely he was feeding her a line. It was tempting to believe him. The flattery gave her ego a much-needed boost. Heaven knew it had taken a beating since Linc had ended their engagement.

"You've gone quiet," he continued. "Don't you believe me?"

"We barely know each other."

"True, but I felt an immediate attraction to you. And I think you noticed the same pull. Why else would you agree to step out of your comfort zone this weekend and come watch me race?"

"Maribelle would've killed me if I'd turned you down." It was a lame cop-out and both of them knew it. London gathered her breath. He'd generously arranged this weekend for her and her friends. She owed him better. "And I wanted to see what you did. Watching you during the practice laps was really exciting."

His full smile nearly blinded her with its brilliance. "Wait until you see the race tomorrow. It gets a lot more interesting when forty guys put it all on the line."

"I imagine it does." She found herself grinning back. His enthusiasm was infectious. "Where are we going?"

While they'd been talking, he'd directed her along the downtown street. Now, as they crossed another street, he gestured her toward a red canopy that marked the entrance to a restaurant.

"The food here is really good. I thought maybe you'd like to try it."

"Lead the way."

He'd brought her to a tiny French bistro with wood floors, a tin ceiling and white linens on the tables. Cozy booths were tucked against a brick wall while the opposite side of the room was lined with bottles of wine. The subdued lighting lent a warm, romantic vibe to the place and the scents filling the air made London's mouth water.

The hostess settled them into a booth near the back where it was quieter and London turned her attention to the menu.

"It all looks so good," she exclaimed. "I don't know what to choose."

"We could order a couple things and share," Harrison suggested.

It would ease the decision-making process, so London nodded. "Since you've been here before, I'm going to let you do the ordering."

"You trust me?"

She somehow sensed he had more on his mind than just meal selection. "Let's just say I'm feeling a little adventurous at the moment."

"I like the sound of that."

After the waitress brought their drinks and left with their orders, London decided to grab the conversational reins.

"So where are you staying?"

"In an RV at the raceway," he replied. "You're welcome to stop by and check it out later. It's pretty roomy with a nice big bed in the back."

"I suppose it makes sense to be close by," she said, ignoring his invitation. "I looked at the weekend schedule and they keep you really busy. I'm surprised you had time to have dinner with me."

"I snuck out," he said with a mischievous grin. "My

uncle thinks I'm going over the data from today's laps before tomorrow's race."

"Really?" She was more than a little shocked until she realized he was kidding. "I'm learning there's a lot more to racing than just getting in a car and going fast."

"Sometimes the tiniest changes can make all the difference."

"So besides making sure you're super-hydrated," she began, referring to the fact that he was only drinking water and wasn't partaking in the bottle of wine he'd ordered for her, "what else goes into preparing for tomorrow's race?" In stark contrast to her earlier skepticism about being interested in a race-car driver, she was finding Harrison's occupation quite interesting.

"I make sure I eat a lot of carbs the night before. I hope you're a fan of chocolate mousse."

"I can always make room for chocolate of any kind."

"Tomorrow morning I'll have a big breakfast followed by a light lunch. In between I'll make sponsor-related appearances before checking in with my crew chief and team to run through last-minute strategy. After that there's a drivers' meeting where the racing association shares information about what's going on that day. If I'm lucky I'll get a few minutes alone at the RV to get my head on straight, but more likely I'll be doing meet and greets. Finally, after lunch, I'll suit up and head to the driver introductions."

"Wow! That's a packed schedule." She was starting to appreciate that his career wasn't just about driving. He was a brand ambassador for his sponsors and the league as well as being a celebrity. "You really don't have any time to yourself."

"Not really. It's all part of the job. And I wouldn't give up any of it."

"You call yourself an introvert, but don't all the public appearances and demands on your time wear you down to nothing?"

"It's not like I don't enjoy meeting my fans." He buttered a piece of bread and popped it into his mouth. "But when I have time off, I make sure I do whatever it takes to reenergize."

"I'm surprised you're out with me, then."

"Are you kidding?" His broad smile dealt her defenses a significant blow. "Being with you is quite exhilarating."

"That's sweet of you to say…"

"I mean it." He gestured at her with another hunk of crusty bread. "And this is where I should probably confess something."

London barely resisted a wince, thinking about her poorly conceived notion to get close to Harrison as a way of getting to his brother. She had yet to figure out what she could do to take Tristan down.

"Like what?" she prompted, hoping it was something terrible so she could feel better about her own questionable morality.

"I used my brother's birthday party as an excuse to see you again."

"Oh." Her pulse skipped. "Does that mean you don't need me as your party planner?" She considered the amount of time she'd spent working on the party and sighed. He wouldn't be the first client to change his mind.

"Not at all. My mother is thrilled that I've taken the project off her hands. My brother can be quite particular when it comes to certain things and it's better if I take the heat for his disappointment."

"You're assuming he'll be disappointed before you've heard any of my plans?" London frowned, but found she wasn't all that insulted. Neither Harrison nor his brother were the toughest clients she'd ever worked for. "That doesn't speak to your faith in my ability to do my job."

Despite the lack of heat or ire in her tone, Harrison's eyes widened. "That's not what I meant at all. I'm sure you will outdo yourself. It's just that Tristan is hard to impress. He's always been that way."

London remembered that Zoe had said something similar about her ex-husband and nodded. "Challenge accepted," she said, digging in where others might throw up their hands and quit.

Harrison nodded. "You thrive under pressure," he said, admiration in his steady gaze. "So do I. It's what makes us good for each other."

Although his words thrilled her, guilt shadowed her delight. Getting revenge on Tristan had prompted her to agree to work on his birthday party and go on that first date with Harrison. She simply had to get her emotions under control.

"You don't think two competitive people will end up ruining things because they're forever chasing the win?" she asked.

"Not if we do it together. I think if we became a team, there's nothing we couldn't accomplish."

Before she started nodding in agreement, London reminded herself of why she'd begun dating him. Getting close to Harrison was a means to an end. And if that made her a terrible person then that was something she'd just have to live with.

Harrison watched his car, number twenty-five, roll into the truck for the return to South Carolina. He was pleased with his second-place finish. With only one race left until the end of the season, he sat in third place for the year and, based on his points, he'd likely hang on to the spot unless he completely screwed up next weekend.

As the car disappeared, a familiar wave of exhaustion swept over him. Once the race was over and the media interviews finished, his body reacted to the long day by shutting down.

"Nice race," his uncle said. The two men were standing side by side while the team rolled Harrison's race car from one set of inspectors to the next. "I was a little worried about you in the beginning."

Today's race had been unusually challenging since at the beginning he'd had to work twice as hard to stay focused on the track and the cars around him while thoughts of London and their dinner last night dominated his mind. Things had gotten better once he'd passed his hundredth lap and settled into the race, needing to win so he could impress London.

"Just wanted to make it interesting," Harrison replied with a sly grin.

"You did that," Jack grumbled. "Let me know when you're ready to head back tonight. I'd like to get out of here by midnight."

"Actually, I've arranged a lift back to Charleston already."

His uncle raised an eyebrow. "Your new girlfriend?"

"She's not my girlfriend...yet." That last word slipped out, revealing something Harrison hadn't yet admitted to himself. He had more than a casual interest in London McCaffrey.

What was going on with him? They'd only been out twice and he was already thinking in terms of a relationship? The only time he was quick to commit was on the track. But when he was with London, their connection felt right and his instincts had never failed him before.

"You sure she's the right woman for you?" his uncle asked, the question a jarring pothole Harrison didn't see coming.

Acid began churning in Harrison's gut. "You have some thoughts on why she isn't?"

While Jack had never commented on any of his drivers' personal lives, he was operating a business where each driver brought in hundreds of thousands to millions of dollars in sponsor revenue each year. That meant he couldn't afford for his team to operate at anything less than 100 percent. And anything that interfered with that would come under fire.

"I asked Dixie about her."

"And?" Harrison challenged.

"She's a social climber." Jack's expression grew hard.

"Apparently she and her mother have been trying to access Charleston inner circles without much success."

"What does that have to do with us dating?" Although he already knew the answer, Harrison wanted to hear his uncle say it.

"I'm just concerned she's going to mess with your head if you're not careful."

"Because I'm not her type?" He'd already figured that out.

"Before Linc Thurston, she'd only gone out with executives and professionals," Jack said. "I don't think she'd have dated a pro ball player if he hadn't belonged to one of Charleston's oldest families. And I'm guessing the reason they're no longer engaged is because Linc figured that out before it was too late."

"I don't think she's as shallow as all that," Harrison said, hoping he was right. "And we're in the early stages of dating. Who's to say where things are going for us."

Jack grunted. "Make sure you figure it out one way or another before the season starts up again in February." His uncle frowned. "I don't need you distracted on the track."

"Hopefully it won't take that long."

Jack nodded and the two men parted ways.

Harrison headed back to the trailer, where he grabbed a quick shower. Even on cooler days like this one, the heat inside the car during the race hovered close to a hundred and thirty degrees. Since the sort of AC in a consumer vehicle weighed too much to be installed in a race car, drivers were cooled by a ventilation system that used hoses and a bag they sat on to blow air on their feet and head. With the average race lasting at least three hours, that was a long time to go without any sort of air-conditioning.

After getting dressed, Harrison slung his duffel over his shoulder and headed to the spot where he'd agreed to meet up with London and her friends. He was intrigued by the fact that Beau had his pilot's license and that Maribelle was learning how to fly. Harrison liked the couple, finding them an upbeat counterpunch to London's reserve.

On the heels of his conversation with Jack, Harrison reflected on his own concerns about what he was getting into with London. If all he wanted was sex, he wasn't going about it the right way given the chemistry that sizzled between them. Take last night, for example. He'd accompanied her back to her hotel room and once again she'd put out a vibe that welcomed physical contact. But instead of backing her into the room and doing all the things he'd been fantasizing about, he'd kissed her on the forehead—not trusting himself to claim her lips—and walked away with an ache in his chest and his loins.

Appreciating the cool night air against his skin, Harrison lengthened his stride, eager to see London and hear her opinion of the race. A silver SUV awaited him near the gate that led to the parking lot. The window was down on the driver's side and Harrison recognized Beau's profile. The easygoing fellow was smiling and gesturing as he spoke to the car's occupants.

"Hey," Harrison said as he approached. "Thanks for the lift."

"Are you kidding?" Beau glanced at his fiancée. "It's the least we could do after the weekend we've had. The behind-the-scenes access you gave us was incredible."

Harrison pulled open the rear driver's-side door and spied London sitting on the far seat. The sight of her made his chest go tight. *Damn.* The woman was beautiful. Today she wore black pants and a denim jacket over a cream sweater. Her hair was bound in a loose braid with long strands framing her pale cheeks. A welcoming smile curved her full, kissable lips and he glimpsed no trace of hesitation in her manner.

Heart thumping erratically, he slid in beside her and became immediately aware of her subtle floral scent. "So what did you think of your first race?" he asked, slipping his duffel into the SUV's cargo area. "Was it what you expected?"

"To be honest, I thought I'd be bored. Five hundred laps seemed like a lot. But it was really fun. It helped to have these two with me." She indicated the couple in the front seats. "They explained a lot of the ins and outs of the strategy. And congratulations on your second-place finish."

"The team had a good weekend," he replied, unsure why he was downplaying his success. Didn't he want to impress this woman? From everything he'd been told, only the best would do for her. "If all goes smoothly next weekend, Crosby Motorsports is poised to finish second this year."

"So next weekend is your last race? What do you do during the off-season?"

"Rest, play and then get ready for next year."

"How much time do you get off to do that?"

"Season starts again in February. I take a break in December to vacation and celebrate the holidays with my family. But even during the off-season I train. Both in the gym and with driving simulations to keep my reflexes sharp." Harrison reached out and took her hand in his, turning it palm up and running the tips of his fingers over her skin. He noticed a slight tremble in her fingers as he caressed her. "I had a really great time last night," he murmured, pitching his voice so only she could hear.

"It was fun. Thank you for dinner." Her gaze flicked from the hand he held to the couple in the front and back to him.

"I'm sorry we had to make such an early night of it."

"You had a big day today. I wouldn't have felt right if I kept you up too late." She sent him a sizzling look from beneath her lashes, banishing his earlier weariness.

Was she feeling bold because they weren't alone?

He toyed with her fingers, imagining how they would feel against his naked body. Yet, to his surprise, the rush of lust such thoughts aroused was matched by a strong craving to find out what made her tick. He lifted her palm to his lips and nipped at her skin. Her sharp gasp made him smile. He'd begun to suspect the route past her defenses might involve keeping her off balance by pushing her sensual boundaries. He would have to test that during tomorrow's hunt for the party venue.

"I think a sleepless night with you would've been worth doing badly today," he murmured.

"I'm sure your uncle wouldn't agree."

"He was young once."

"He's running a multimillion-dollar racing team," she countered, her tone tart. "And even if he forgave you, what about your sponsors?"

Harrison let loose an exaggerated sigh. "One of these days you're going to surprise me by not being so practical."

"You think so?" A faint smile curved her lips.

"I know so."

London subsided into reflective silence for several minutes and Harrison gave her room to think. At long last she said, "It's not part of my nature to be rash and spontaneous. My mother drilled into my head that I should think first and act second. She's very concerned with appearances, and growing up, I never had an opportunity to spread my wings, so to speak."

This bit of insight into her past intrigued him. "What would you have done if your choices hadn't been so restricted?"

"Run off and join the circus?" Her weak attempt at humor was obviously an attempt to deflect his probing. After a second she gave a half-hearted shrug and said, "I don't know. Sometimes I resent that my mother was so obsessed with advancing my position in Charleston society."

"Only sometimes?" he challenged.

London's fingers briefly tightened over his. "When I let myself think about it." For a long moment she sat in silence, but soon his patience was rewarded. "It's hard when your mother thinks your worth is defined by who you marry. That's something other people judge you by, not your own parent."

"Why do you care?"

His blunt question apparently surprised her. Despite the shadowy confines of the back seat, he could easily read the sudden tension in her expression.

She reacted as if he'd attacked some core value she lived by. "I want her to be glad I'm her daughter."

Harrison understood why this was important. Tristan had long sought their father's approval, especially since taking over Crosby Automotive. Harrison's brother seemed obsessed with matching the success their father had made of the company, yet profits had been mostly flat in the first few years Tristan had been in charge. Still, that hadn't seemed to affect his personal spending. Something Harrison had heard his uncle criticize more than once.

"You don't think she admires all you've accomplished?" Harrison asked, returning his thoughts to London's situation.

"I think my dad does." Pride glowed in her voice. "My company is very successful and that makes him proud."

"But not your mother?"

"She might've been happy if I'd married Linc and had several boys and one girl."

"Why only one girl?" Harrison suspected he knew the answer before she spoke.

"Obviously my mother's opinion is that women are worth less than men." London's tone was more matter-of-fact than bitter. "Still, she'd like to have a granddaughter who could do what I couldn't. Become a debutante."

Harrison knew his mother had gone through the classes and been presented at nineteen. But in this day and age, did that stuff even matter?

"Why is it so important to her?" he asked.

"My mother grew up in New York City and was never selected for the International Debutante Ball there, despite her family's connections and wealth. She took the rejection hard." London shifted in her seat, turning to face him. "And then she gets to Charleston and finds all the doors are closed to her. No one cared about her money. All that mattered was she was from *off*." London freed her hand briefly so she could form air quotes around the last word.

"You should talk to my mother," Harrison said. "She rejected becoming a debutante and married my dad, who was not only an outsider but poor by her family standards."

"I'm going to guess she'd tell me to follow my heart?"

"That was the advice she gave me when my dad hassled me about choosing racing over working for Crosby Automotive. If I hadn't, I'd be working for the family business and completely miserable."

"You don't see yourself as a businessman?"

"Honestly, not the sort who sits in an office and stares at reports all day. My plan is to take over for my uncle one day and run Crosby Motorsports."

"And in the meantime you're just going to race and have fun."

"Nothing wrong with having fun. I'd like to demonstrate that to you."

"What sort of fun do you think I'd be interested in?" she asked, her manner serious rather than flirtatious.

"Hard to say until I get to know you better." He had several ideas on the subject. "But would you have guessed that you'd enjoy today's race as much as you did?"

"No, not really. Maybe I do need to look outside my limited circle of activities."

"So that's a yes to new experiences?"

"As long as you're willing to balance adventure with somewhat tamer forms of entertainment," she said, "I'm in."

No sweeter words had ever been spoken by a woman.

Six

Shortly after lunch on the Monday following her weekend in Richmond, London sat at her desk, doodling on her notepad, her cell phone on speaker while Maribelle went on and on about how much she and Beau had enjoyed their time at the raceway. London's attention, however, was not on the race but on the man who'd invited her to it.

Almost as if her friend could read her mind, Maribelle said, "He's really into you. I think that's so great."

Maribelle's remark sent a little shiver of pleasure through London. "I don't know what to think."

But she wasn't being completely truthful. London was in fact thinking that she'd intended to use Harrison to get close to his brother, and the more time she spent with the race-car driver, the more troubling her attraction to him became.

Despite their closeness, London hadn't told Maribelle about the crazy plan hatched at the Beautiful Women Taking Charge event. London knew if she looked too deeply at why she'd kept it from her best friend of fifteen years, doubts would surface about her moral choices. Shame flooded her as London realized how far she'd strayed from the person she'd believed herself to be. Yet to stop now when others were depending on her...

"Are you worried what your mother would think of him?" Maribelle asked, breaking into London's thoughts.

Maribelle had been there for London during high school when Edie Fremont-McCaffrey's frustration with Charleston's society rules had made London's life hell. It wasn't her fault that she wasn't allowed to be a debutante, but that hadn't stopped her mother from raining criticisms down on her daughter's head. Blaming her mother gave London an excuse to be conflicted about getting involved with Harrison so that her real concerns never had to surface.

"She wasn't exactly thrilled with the fact that Linc was a professional baseball player, but he was wealthy and had the old Charleston social connections that she wanted for me." London toyed with her earring. "Can you imagine how she'd feel about Harrison? Not only is he a race-car driver, but his father and uncle are from off with no social standing."

"Why do you care?"

It wasn't the first time Maribelle had asked the question. Nor did it spark the familiar surge of resentment that was always just below the surface. About how easy it was for someone who had it all to downplay their advantages. Add to that how supportive Maribelle's family was about everything she did, and bitterness had often colored London's mood. Today, however, London was feeling less defensive than usual.

"Because fighting her is so much work. It's easier to give in." The admission flowed from London's lips, startling her. And apparently surprising Maribelle, as well, because for a long few seconds neither woman spoke.

"Oh, London."

Sudden tears erupted in London's eyes. Shocked by the rush of emotion, she blinked rapidly, determined not to give in. Her mother had hounded her mercilessly all her life and London had always braced against it. For as long as she could remember, London had maintained a resilient facade while secretly believing that Edie was right and it was all London's fault.

She picked up the phone and took it off speaker. "My mother is a tyrant," she said in a barely audible whisper, almost as if she was afraid to voice what was in her heart. "She has criticized nearly everything I've ever done or said."

"She's a terrible person," Maribelle agreed, always London's champion. "But she's also your mother and you want to please her. It's normal."

But was it? Shouldn't parents want what was best for their children? That being said, Edie would claim that encouraging her daughter to marry well was the most important thing for London's future, but it was pretty clear that her mother didn't take London's happiness into account, as well.

"Maybe I need a new normal," London groused.

"Maybe you do," Maribelle said, her tone deadly serious. "What are you wearing right now?"

The question came out of nowhere and made London laugh. She dabbed at the trace of moisture lingering near the corner of her eye and found her spirits rising.

"Are you trying to get me to engage in phone sex with you?" London teased, pretending to sound outraged. "Because I don't think either of us rolls that way."

"Ha, ha," Maribelle sounded more impatient than amused. "I'm only asking because I heard you making plans to get together with Harrison today to go venue shopping. I hope you're wearing something less…reserved than usual."

London glanced down at the emerald green wrap dress she wore. The style was more fun and relaxed than her typical uniform of conservative suits in understated shades of gray, blue and black.

"I'm wearing the necklace you bought me for Christmas last year." London had not previously worn the statement necklace of stone flowers in hot jewel tones, thinking the look was too bold for her. But today she'd wanted her appearance to make an impact and the necklace had paired perfectly with the dress.

"Is your hair up?"

London's fingers automatically went to the sleek side bun she wore.

"Forget I asked," Maribelle said. "Just take it down and send me a picture."

Feeling slightly ridiculous, London did as she was told, even going so far as to fluff her blond waves into a sexy, disheveled look, and was rewarded by her friend's joyful squeal.

"I think that means you approve."

"This is the London McCaffrey I've been waiting for all my life," Maribelle declared in rapturous tones. "You look fantastic and it's so nice to see you ditching those dull duds you think make you look professional."

"Thanks?" Despite her friend's backhanded compliment, London was feeling optimistic and excited about seeing Harrison again. Would he approve of her new look? Or was he a typical guy who wouldn't notice?

"You really like him, don't you?"

London opened her mouth, preparing to deny the way her heart raced and nerves danced whenever she was with Harrison, but couldn't lie to her friend. "I do like him. More than I expected to. That being said, it might be that we have a lot of chemistry and there's no possible way we're compatible beyond that." She left an unspoken *but* hanging in the air.

It was getting harder and harder to make excuses for why dating Harrison would be a waste of her time. Unfortunately, the real reason was a secret London could never share with her friend and that made what she was doing all the worse.

"Say whatever you want," Maribelle said. "But I see things working out between you two."

"I don't know. We're so different. We have divergent

points of view about lifestyle and the things we enjoy. How do we go forward if we have nothing in common?"

"That sounds like your mother talking. How different are you really? You both come from money. You may not run in the same groups, but your families share some social connections. Both of you are committed to your careers and highly competitive. If you're talking about the fact that he races cars for a living, he makes a boatload of money doing it and I think you'd be bored with some stuffy businessman who only wants to talk about how his company is doing. You need someone who gets you riled up."

"You keep saying things like that, but excitement has never been my criterion for finding a man attractive before."

"How's that worked out for you thus far?"

Before London could protest that she was quite happy with her life, her desk phone lit up with a call from Missy, likely indicating that Harrison had arrived.

"I think Harrison's here."

"Call me later to let me know how it went."

Instead of reminding her friend that this was a business meeting, London said, "I'm sure there won't be anything to tell."

"Let me be the judge of that."

London was shaking her head as she disconnected with her friend and answered the call from her receptionist. Sure enough, Harrison was waiting for her in the lobby.

Before she picked up her tablet containing all the information on the four venues she'd be showing Harrison today, London double-checked her makeup and applied a fresh coat of lipstick. She noted her sparkling eyes and the flush over her cheekbones put there in anticipation of seeing Harrison. The man had certainly gotten beneath her skin. Worse, she was glad of it.

Despite the fact that she'd seen him the night before, London's stomach flipped as she walked into the reception area and spied Harrison's tall figure. Although her primping had kept him waiting, he wasn't checking his phone or flirting with her receptionist. Instead he was focused on the hallway leading to her office. Their eyes collided and a shower of sparks raced across London's nerve endings, leaving her breathless and light-headed.

"Hi," she said, her voice sounding not at all professional. Cursing her body's longing to fling itself against his, she cleared her throat and tried again. "Sorry I kept you waiting." Flustered by his slow, sexy smile, she turned to the receptionist. "Missy, I'll be gone for the rest of the afternoon. See you in the morning."

"Sure." Missy brazenly winked at her. "You two have fun now."

London's mouth dropped open and her brain was scrambling to come up with something to reply when Harrison caught her hand and tugged her toward the door. She noticed how the man smelled delicious as he guided her to his Mercedes.

"Where to first?" he asked as he slid behind the wheel.

Although the entire afternoon's plans were already firmly in her mind, she cued up her tablet, needing something to do to avoid looking at him. After naming an address half a mile down on King Street, she began listing the positives and negatives of the space.

"The best part is their menu. They have an excellent chef. Unfortunately, there is no elevator, so the space is only accessible by stairs. I only mention it in case you have any guests who can't make the climb."

"That shouldn't be a problem."

Harrison found an open spot along the curb a half block up from their destination and parked. They then walked back toward the venue. As Harrison held the front door, allowing her to pass, she noticed his slight frown. The first floor of the narrow building was occupied by a wine bar.

"Don't let the size down here fool you," she said, waving at the manager. "Upstairs is fifteen hundred square feet and feels much more open and airy. There's plenty of room for all your guests and even an outdoor patio if the night is mild." She broke off to greet Jim Gleeson and introduced the manager to Harrison. "Jim has helped me with several corporate functions over the last two years," she explained.

The two men shook hands and then Jim led the way upstairs. "We can set up the space however you envision it," the manager said over his shoulder. "And the room is big enough that we can divide it into a cocktail setting with high tables or couches on one end and large round tables on the other for dinner."

"I think that would be nice," London said.

They'd reached the second floor and Harrison wasn't evaluating the space, but rather, his attention was focused on her.

"Since we'd talked about a jazz band," she continued, determined to treat him like a client in this setting, "we could place them near the bar as people first enter."

At the moment the room was set up for a cocktail party with a freestanding bar at each end and high-top tables scattered along the perimeter.

Jim's phone buzzed and he excused himself, leaving the pair alone.

Somehow as soon as it was just the two of them, the massive room became oddly intimate. Or maybe it was the way Harrison was looking at her as if he intended to penetrate her professional mask and get to the woman beneath. London couldn't stop herself from recalling how disappointed she'd been on Saturday night that he hadn't tried to kiss her good-night. Or the way they'd leaned toward each other on the plane ride back, sharing the armrest as he'd shown her the camera footage from inside his race car.

"What I really like here is all the period details," she began, taking refuge in professionalism to avoid Harrison's hot gaze. She walked away from him, gesturing at the exposed brick and white wainscoting. Her heels clicked on the polished pine floor and echoed off the gleaming wood in the original coffered ceiling. "Isn't this fireplace fantastic?"

"I think you're fantastic."

"I'm picturing ten tables of ten. With big glass vases holding candles and filled with glass beads in the center. Since it's December, we could do evergreen centerpieces, but maybe that's too predictable." Aware that she was rambling, London continued. To stop meant she might give in to the longing pulsing through her. "Or we could do glass pillars with layered candies like peppermints and foil-wrapped chocolates in red and green. Unless you think he's too sophisticated and would prefer crystal with white and silver."

While she'd been going on and on, Harrison had been stalking after her, his expression intent, his gaze narrowed. Now, as she approached the door leading out to the rooftop patio, he set his hand on the doorknob before she could reach it, halting her retreat.

"I think you're fantastic," he repeated, compelling her to stop dodging him. "Everything about you interests me."

"I like you a lot," she admitted, surprising both of them with the confession. "What you do is dangerous and exciting. I never imagined..."

Oh, what was she doing? It was on the tip of her tongue to spill everything about the riotous, treacherous emotions driving her actions. To share how disappointed she'd been Saturday night because he hadn't tried anything when he'd brought her back to her hotel room. Confessing her developing feelings for him was the absolute wrong thing to do. So how was she supposed to get out of the verbal corner she'd backed herself into?

Harrison watched a dozen conflicting emotions race across London's features. Most of the time she'd demonstrated a sphinxian ability to keep her thoughts concealed. Her need to keep herself hidden frustrated him. He wanted her to open up and share what made her tick.

"I've also had great success with hurricane holders filled with rice lights and Christmas balls," she stated in a breathless rush, returning to the earlier topic of center-pieces. "Or glass bowls with candles floating above holly sprigs."

"Never imagined what?" Harrison prompted, ignoring her attempt to evade the real subject.

She shook her head. "This really isn't the place for this conversation."

"Where would you like to go?" He hoped she'd suggest her place. Or his. It was past time he got her alone.

"I set aside my afternoon to help you find a venue for your brother's birthday party."

"London," he murmured, cradling her head in his palm, thumb caressing her flushed cheek.

"Yes?"

Her voice was equally soft and it seemed to him a trace of desperation colored her tone as if with each thump of her heart she was losing the fight to maintain control. It echoed how he felt when they were together. Each moment in her company tested his willpower. He knew better than to pressure her like this. As much as he wanted to go in with guns blazing, she needed to be coaxed. Wooed. Enticed. But damn if he didn't want to feel her surrender beneath his touch.

"I don't really care what venue we choose," he said. "The only reason I'm here today is to spend time with you."

He placed just the tips of his fingers on her spine. A tremor went through her an instant before she tipped her head back and gazed up at his face. The hunger glowing in her eyes transfixed him. Inching closer, he dipped his head until he could feel her breath on his skin. He grazed his nose against hers, ending the move with a slight bump that nudged her head into a better angle. Smiling at the sigh that escaped her, he slanted his mouth above hers, not quite making contact. Although he'd already kissed her on the street in downtown Charleston, that location hadn't offered him the privacy to do it right. Plus, it had been too soon to take things as far as he wanted to.

This time it would be different.

She made a soft impatient noise in the seconds before their lips met and his world stopped being ordinary. Then another sound erupted from her throat as fire flashed through him. Wildness sped across his nerve endings, setting his heart to pounding. Endless fantasies of her and him naked and rolling over his mattress in hungry, frenzied passion flashed through his mind.

Harrison didn't give a damn that the manager might return and interrupt them. The only thing on his mind was the woman making his heart pound and his body heat. Longing had gotten hold of him and wouldn't let go.

With one hand coaxing her forward, bringing her torso into contact with chest and abs, he cupped her cheek with the other and deepened the kiss. It nearly killed him to go slow when he wanted so much more. Her lips. Tongue. Teeth. All of her. And when her lips parted and a soft, helpless groan escaped her, he nearly lost his mind.

In the instant her body melted into his, they were

both swept up in a way that Harrison found himself powerless to stop. Despite his best intentions, the kiss went nova too fast for him to rein it in. Instead he surrendered the fight, realizing while he desired this woman more with each encounter, she wanted him just as much.

This was how a kiss was supposed to be. A give-and-take of sweetness and lust. Pure longing and dirty intentions. He slid his tongue across hers, claiming her mouth and driving her passion harder. Her fingers clutched his hair and dented his leather jacket. It was all crazy, frantic fun with a poignant dash of inevitability, and he never wanted it to end.

The sound of footsteps on the wooden stairs behind him jolted Harrison back to reality. Cursing inwardly, he broke off the kiss and gulped in air. Without releasing his hold on London, he blinked several times in rapid succession, trying to reorient himself to their surroundings. When had he ever lost control like that? Who was this woman who could make him go crazy by relating details about square footage, color schemes and table layouts?

"How are we doing?" came a bright voice from the far end of the room.

London jerked in response to the interruption and pulled Harrison's hand from her face. She took a half step back, her eyes stunned and wide as they met his. Her chest rose and fell as she put her hand to her mouth, hiding a dismayed *oh*. Harrison surveyed the hot color of her skin and her passion-bruised lips, unable to resist a smile.

Damn, she looked gorgeous with her vulnerability on display. All softness and submission. But even as this thought registered in his mind, he could tell she was rapidly regaining her poise. Her features shifted into the cool reserve with which she confronted the world. Only her eyes betrayed her in the second before her lashes dipped, concealing her confusion.

"It all looks great," he called to the manager. "I think we'll take it."

"Great," the man replied. "I'll get the paperwork started."

"You go do that," Harrison said. "We have a few more things to talk about up here and then we'll be down."

"I have three more properties to show you," London reminded him in a harsh whisper, regaining her voice even as the manager's footsteps retreated down the stairs. "You can't make a decision without seeing all of them."

He skimmed his fingertips over her cheekbone, admiring her delicate bone structure. "Do you really want to spend the rest of the afternoon pretending to look at properties while what we really want to do is get to know each other better?"

"I…" Her eyes narrowed. "If you think one kiss means I'm going to sleep with you, you're wrong."

No doubt she'd intended to make this declaration in tart tones, but her voice had lacked conviction.

"You have a dirty mind," he scolded, giving her an affectionate tap on her perfect nose. "I like that in a woman."

"I don't have anything of the sort."

"Really?" He raised an eyebrow. "I say I want to get to know you better and you assume that means sex."

"Well, sure." She gnawed on her lip and frowned. "I mean…"

"Table that thought," he growled, dropping his head and giving her a firm, brief kiss on the lips. "What I meant by getting to know each other better was more about how you came to Richmond this weekend to watch me race. I thought it might be nice for you to show me a little of your world."

It had occurred to him after being dropped off the night before that London McCaffrey had learned way more about him than he'd discovered about her.

Her gaze remained glued to him as she gestured toward the room. "This is it."

"What? Do you mean work? There has to be more to your life than just this." When she shook her head, Harrison nodded. Obviously they were two of a kind when it came to their careers. "So we'll continue to plan the party. We've chosen a venue. What's next?"

"The menu. Flowers. Invitations. A theme."

A theme? Harrison kept his thoughts hidden with some difficulty as he imagined the challenge in finding something that would appeal to his brother. Maybe his mother would have some ideas.

"So, let's go downstairs, sign the contract, plan the meal and then go buy some flowers."

She regarded him skeptically. "Really? You want to do that?"

"I want to spend time with you and see what you

enjoy doing. If that involves flowers and invitations, so be it."

For several heartbeats she remained undecided, but instead of pushing, Harrison stayed silent and let her sort through whatever it was she was grappling with. At last she nodded.

"But first," he said, turning her around until they were both staring through the glass door leading outside. "Let's talk about this patio."

"Okay."

Her expression as she glanced back at him reflected her puzzlement. Keeping her off balance was part of his plan to discover all the little things she kept concealed.

"How do you see us using the space for Tristan's party?" As he spoke, he grabbed her wrists and slid her hands to the wood portion of the door before pushing her palms flat against the narrow panel. "Keep your hands right there. Now, tell me your thoughts."

She shivered as he ran his hands up her arms to her shoulders before moving aside her hair, exposing her neck. "They can string lights and put out couches."

"What else?"

He dusted a kiss just below her hairline, hearing her breath stutter as his lips continued to play over the fragrant flesh of her neck and run along the neckline of her dress. He dipped beneath the fabric with his finger, baring the top of her spine, claiming her shoulder, collarbone and nape with soft kisses.

She pushed back into his body and moaned as her backside came into contact with his erection. The sound inflamed his already fiery desire and he murmured encouragement as he kissed the shell of her ear and nipped at her earlobe.

"What else?" he repeated. "How do you envision the scene?"

"Um," she said, her breath coming faster. "We could have them set up a bar. Oh, that feels good."

This last was in response to his hand sliding over her stomach and splaying as she rocked her hips, rubbing herself against him.

"How many people do you think could fit out there?" he quizzed, dipping his hand beneath the hem of her dress and running his fingertips up her thigh.

"A couple dozen. Oh." Her head fell back against his shoulder as he grazed the inside of her thigh. "What you're doing to me..."

"Yes?" he prompted.

Did she have any idea she'd parted her legs to give him better access? He raked her neck with his teeth, dying to touch her, to find out if she was wet for him.

"Don't stop."

"Besides the lights and couches, how would you decorate?"

He ran his fingers over the cotton panel of her panties, noting the damp fabric.

"Please." She was panting and rocking against his hand, making low, incoherent noises, trying to ask for more.

"How would you decorate?" he repeated, sliding his fingers beneath he elastic of her panties and cupping her for a long second before dipping his finger into her wetness. With a heartfelt groan he stroked her, absorb-

ing her shudders as he discovered just how she liked
to be touched.

"Candles." She ejected the word like a curse. "Lots
and lots and lots of candles."

She was coming. Hard. Her hips rocked and bucked
as her spine arched. The sounds emanating from her
stopped being coherent. A storm was rising and it fed
his own pleasure. In that moment they were no longer two people but one being, both focused on driving
her into a mind-blowing orgasm. And then he felt the
first wave of it rush over her. Felt her start to shatter
against him.

"Give it to me, baby," he said. "Let me take care of
you."

Her nails dug into his thigh. He'd been so focused on
her he hadn't even realized she'd gripped him there. But
now her touch, so close to his aching erection, caused
him to harden to the point of pain.

"Oh, Harrison."

Her words ended in a shudder that seemed endless
as she climaxed and he held on, easing his strokes as
the last of her pleasure dimmed. Panting and limp, head
bowed, she braced herself with one hand on the door
frame and sucked great gulps of air into her lungs. The
other hand eased its death grip on his thigh and she
pushed a lock of hair behind her ear.

"God, I love making you come," he murmured, easing his hand from between her legs. He placed his palm
on her stomach, keeping their bodies together while he
dipped his head and kissed her neck.

"Not as much as I love coming," she retorted with a shaky chuckle.

He found his breath wasn't altogether steady as he said, "I've never known anyone like you."

"Really?" Her head swiveled just enough to give him a glimpse of her skeptical expression.

"Really."

Beneath her show of reserve—and he now realized that was all it was, a performance she'd played all her life—lurked a wild woman, unsatisfied with all the restrictions placed on her by society and expectations. He looked forward to coaxing her from hiding.

"You haven't gotten other women off in public?"

"Most of the women I've been with know the score. They're with me because of who I am and are willing to do whatever I'm into." He turned her around and put his hands on her shoulders, waiting until she met his gaze before continuing. "You are with me in spite of who I am. What just happened was all about you. For you. I'm incredibly honored just to be a part of it."

"I can't believe I did that," she murmured, disbelief in her tone. "That wasn't at all like me."

"I think it was. You just don't want to admit it." He paused a beat, noted that she remained unsure and finished, "You were incredible."

"Don't expect that it will happen again."

But they both knew it wasn't the end. He recognized the truth in his gut and saw acknowledgment in her eyes.

"Whatever you want to happen will."

And as she frowned at him, trying to interpret what he meant, Harrison knew that party planning had never been so sexy.

Seven

Chip Corduroy was the sort of Charleston insider London had begun cultivating long before she'd started her event planning business because he knew everyone's dirty secrets and could be counted on to trade information for favors. The slender fifty-year-old had a proud pedigree and expensive taste. Unfortunately, that meant he mostly lived above his means, which was why he loved that London "treated" him to spa days, shopping excursions and dinners out at the best restaurants in exchange for leads and introductions.

"I heard you've been out with Harrison Crosby a few times," Chip said, shooting her a sideways glance.

They were standing in front of the hostess at Felix Cocktails et Cuisine waiting to be seated and London wasn't at all surprised that the sandy-haired man had caught wind of their dates.

"It's business," she responded, keeping her answers short. "I'm planning his brother's birthday party."

"Doesn't really seem your type," Chip persisted, obviously not believing her explanation.

"Because he's a race-car driver?" She heard the defensive note in her voice and inwardly winced.

"Because his family isn't old Charleston."

"There aren't many eligible men who are." London sighed, feeling disingenuous as she fed Chip what he expected her to say. "But from everything I've heard, it seems as if Tristan and I would be better suited." The lie tasted awful on her tongue, but she needed whatever Chip knew about Tristan.

"So you've given up on getting back together with Linc?" From the routine nature of the question, London suspected he already knew the answer. "I mean, you two were the golden couple."

"Maybe on paper."

In truth, the longer they'd been together and the more interest Linc had displayed in settling down and starting a family, the more she'd dragged her feet about setting a wedding date. Frankly, she'd been terrified at the idea that she'd be expected to give up her career and had struggled to imagine herself as a mother. Did she have the patience for children? Or the interest?

And yet none of those same questions or insecurities bombarded her when she imagined herself with Harrison. Not that she saw a future with him. Her mother would disown her if London married a race-car driver.

And then there was the revenge plot against Tristan, something she'd have to keep secret from Harrison forever. What chance did a relationship have when the partners weren't truthful with each other?

No doubt the impossibility of a happily-ever-after with Harrison was what kept her anxieties at bay. Convinced they had no future, London was free to daydream about them settling into a house somewhere between downtown Charleston and the Crosby Motorsports complex. With her business growing ever more successful each year and thanks to the hard work of the fantastic staff she'd hired, she was in a position where she could delegate more. They'd have two darling kids. A boy and a girl. Both would have Harrison's sea green eyes and her blond hair. They would grow up to become anything they wanted to be with both parents encouraging their individual interests.

"Have you heard that he's taken up with his housekeeper?" Chip asked, dragging London away from her daydream.

She found herself reluctant to emerge from the satisfying fantasy. "Really?" She forced herself to sound aghast, knowing it would spur her companion to greater gossip even as her actions filled her with distaste.

"He's definitely sleeping with her."

When his mother had encouraged Linc to hire Claire Robbins, London's initial reaction had been to doubt Maribelle's concerns that the pretty military widow was competition and to ignore the fact that Claire and Linc had chemistry. In London's view, Claire was obviously still in love with her deceased husband and utterly focused on her darling toddler.

"Has he come out and said so?" London asked, breaking her promise to not dabble in unsubstantiated rumor about her ex. "Or is that just speculation?"

"They've been going out to dinner and he bought her a pair of earrings." Chip declared this as if it definitively proved his claim. "And the way he looked at her at his mother's party?" Chip fanned himself even as he rolled his eyes emphatically. "There's definitely something going on."

"That's all speculation," she insisted, hoping the gossip wasn't true. Something about Claire was off. She'd been too evasive when discussing her life before Charleston. "Plus, even if he's sleeping with her, it's not going to last."

Chip looked shocked. "Well, of course not."

As the hostess led them to a table, London shoved all thoughts of her ex to the back burner. Linc was Everly's project and London needed to give every appearance of having moved on to avoid any backlash after Everly's revenge plan came to fruition.

As London settled into her seat, she scrambled for a way to shift the conversation to what Chip knew about Tristan Crosby. When no smooth segue came to mind, she decided to be forthright.

"Harrison hired me to plan a surprise birthday party for his brother. What can you tell me about Tristan?"

Chip leveled a speculative look on her before answering. "Dresses well. Loves the finest money can buy. Gives to charities, but not because he cares, more so people will tell him how great he is. Several women have told me he's a sexual predator. Don't let yourself be alone with him or he'll have his hands all over you."

None of this was news, so she pushed for more. "Wasn't he married until recently?"

"Zoe. Nice girl. She had no idea what she was getting into when she married him."

"Girl?" London echoed, picturing the woman she'd met weeks earlier. "I thought she was in her late twenties."

"I'm speaking figuratively. He snapped her up when she was still in college and she always seemed to have a deer-in-the-headlights look about her. She barely spoke when they were out together. Just a decorative bit of arm candy that every guy in the room wanted as their own."

London shuddered as she pondered how it would feel to be valued for her face and figure alone. Although she'd barely met Zoe, their shared experience of personally being wronged by powerful, wealthy men had given her a sense of sisterhood that she hadn't felt with Everly, whose beef with Ryan Dailey had to do with his treatment of her sister.

"You can do better," Chip said, redirecting her attention. "Might I suggest Grady Edwards? Good family. Wealthy. A little obsessed with polo for my taste, but no one is perfect."

"I'll keep him in mind," London replied diplomatically, struggling for a way to return the conversation to Tristan. "Although I heard Landry Beaumont has been seeing him." This was a spurious remark. Rumor had it

Landry was chasing Linc. "So what happened between Tristan Crosby and his ex-wife?"

"He dumped her. Something about her having an affair. Later I heard he fabricated the whole thing to get out of paying her anything. The man is ruthless," Chip said, leaning forward and lowering his voice conspiratorially even though no one was close enough to hear their conversation. "Magnolia Spencer told me in confidence that Zoe got next to nothing."

"Because of a prenup?"

"Because there's no money."

"How is that possible? Crosby Automotive does exceptionally well and, from what I hear, Tristan has been remodeling the Theodore Norwood house on Montague for the last five years. A client of mine has done some of the work and said Tristan has put nearly three million into the project."

Chip shrugged as he eyed the menu. The restaurant was known for its creative cocktails and small plates all done with a Parisian flare. "What looks good?"

As much as London wanted to keep the conversation alive, she decided more digging would only make Chip suspicious. Whatever Tristan was doing, his activities weren't spawning the sort of gossip that if it got out might harm him.

London stared at the menu, but her thoughts were far away. Finding an indirect way to take down Tristan seemed impossible.

Zoe had explained that Tristan was incredibly secretive about his finances. So much so that when her divorce lawyer had looked into his assets, it had become pretty obvious that Tristan spent far more than his annual salary from Crosby Automotive and the income he received from his investments.

"I think I'm going to have the tarte flambée," Chip said. "Or maybe the Spanish octopus."

Decisions made, London settled back and listened with half her attention as Chip filled her in on all the latest events. She let her troubling thoughts about Tristan drift to Harrison and the risky path she was following.

What had happened between them at the venue where his brother's party would be held was a perfect example of what a mistake it was to become involved with Harrison. The man held an unexpected and compelling power over her libido. She still couldn't believe she'd had an orgasm like that in a public place where at any moment they could be discovered.

Her cheeks went hot as she recalled how she'd rocked and writhed against him, greedily grabbing at the pleasure he'd offered. She'd never climaxed like that before, and recognized that some of her excitement had come from the danger of being caught with his hand up her skirt.

When London had shared what had happened with Maribelle, her friend had at first been shocked and then wildly encouraging. To say that London had stepped outside her comfort zone was a major understatement. What surprised her almost more than letting Harrison touch her like that was her lack of regret in the aftermath. She'd done something wicked and wanton and failed to hear her mother's voice rain scathing recriminations down upon her head. Maybe she was making progress.

London's phone buzzed. It was Thursday evening and Harrison had flown to Miami for the last race of the season. She was a little shocked the way her heart jumped in anticipation of hearing from him. Still, she left the phone screen down on the table.

Following that incredible encounter on Monday afternoon, Harrison had been a man of his word and accompanied her to choose flowers and pick out stationery.

In the subsequent days, even though he'd been preoccupied with pre-race preparations, he'd sent her several charming messages that made her body sing.

With each text she'd grown more and more impatient to see him again. She caught herself daydreaming about what she would do the next time she got him alone. In all-too-brief moments of clarity, London reminded herself that this behavior ran counter to her real purpose in getting to know him better. She was supposed to be focused on securing whatever information she could to take down his brother. The push and pull of regret and longing was making her question her character and decisions.

Unfortunately, it was too late to back out now.

Her phone buzzed again.

"Do you need to get that?" Chip asked.

Fighting the need to connect with Harrison was too much work and London nodded with relief. "It might be work," she said, hoping that wasn't the case.

It's hot in Miami. Thinking of you in a bikini.

Joy blasted through her, shocking in its power. Giddy with delight, she forgot that she was sitting across from one of Charleston's most fervent gossips.

Missing you.

She stared at the words she'd just sent. Despite the fact that it was true, she couldn't believe she'd opened herself up like that.

You're sure you can't join me?

She bit her lip as temptation raged within her. The corporate event she'd arranged for Saturday night could be turned over to Grace. It would be so easy to jump on a plane and be in the stands cheering him on Sunday afternoon.

Can't. How about dinner Monday? My place.

His response came at her in a flash.

Sure.

She sent a smiley face emoji and returned the phone to the table, aware she was smirking. Only then did she glance at her dinner companion and notice that he wore a bemused expression.

"That wasn't work," Chip said.

"What makes you say that?" she hedged, a flush racing over her skin.

"I've never seen you smile like that before." His eyes narrowed. "Not even when you were first engaged to Linc. You are glowing. Who is he?"

London shook her head. "What makes you think it was a he? It could've been Maribelle."

"It was Harrison Crosby, wasn't it?" Chip countered, displaying absolute confidence in his deductive reasoning. "You're interested in him. He's a catch."

"Is he?" London replied weakly, "I guess I haven't thought of him that way."

Lies, lies, all lies. She'd thought of little else these last few days. London was abruptly appalled at the person she was becoming. Nor did she have a plan to extricate herself from her pledge to take down Tristan even as her feelings for Harrison grew. More and more she was convinced that everything was going to blow up in her face and her actions would end up causing harm rather than helping Zoe.

At a table near the front window of the coffee shop across the street from London's ExcelEvent office, Everly sipped green tea and pondered her ever-deepening concern over London's relationship with Harrison. Stupid idiot. At least she'd picked the inconsequential brother to fall for. Everly would have to kill her if she'd fallen for Tristan.

Her cell buzzed, indicating an incoming call from her assistant. Annoyed with the distraction, she sent the call to voice mail. She refused to make London's mistake and lose focus. A second later her phone buzzed again. It was Nora again.

Blowing out a breath, she unclenched her teeth and answered. "What?"

"Devon Connor is here for your four o'clock meeting," Nora said, unruffled by her employer's sharp tone.

"What four o'clock meeting?"

Everly handled the branding for his numerous golf resorts up and down the coast. In the year since Kelly had been arrested, his account had become the bulk of her business.

"The one I texted and called and emailed you about yesterday and this morning. Where are you?"

Everly silently cursed. "Tell him I've been delayed."

"How long?"

A quick glance at her watch showed it was a quarter past four already. London usually left work by now.

Earlier today Everly had secured a little bit of tech that could help them all out. After deciding London was neither computer savvy enough nor equipped with the right tools to get dirt on Tristan Crosby, Everly had taken matters into her own hands.

The USB drive in her purse had come from a source connected to a friend of her sister's. In college Kelly had run with a group that hacked for fun. Everly hadn't known about it at the time or she'd have warned Kelly away from such recklessness.

The drive contained software that, when plugged into a computer and with a few commands, could bypass passwords and copy everything on the hard drive. The question remained if London was up to the challenge of gaining access to Tristan's computer.

"Reschedule him for tomorrow," Everly said, calculating how much work remained on the presentation for his newest acquisition. "Or if you can push him to next week that would be even better."

"He's not going to be happy."

"Make something up. Tell him I'm dealing with an emergency." Everly spotted London exiting her office. "I have to go."

Hanging up on her assistant, Everly exited the coffee shop and followed London, doing her best to behave like an unremarkable woman window-shopping along King Street.

London walked briskly. Obviously she had some place to be. Rushing off to another date with Harrison, no doubt. The thought made Everly grind her teeth.

Honestly, what did London think she was doing? Did the event planner imagine she and Harrison had any sort of chance? Even if London was merely engaging in a bit of fun with the handsome race-car driver, her priorities were skewed. Irritation flared that Everly needed to remind her of this fact again.

London had almost reached her car. Everly lengthened her stride until she was jogging and her timing was perfect. As London pushed the unlock button on her key fob, Everly drew within several feet of her.

"Where are you running off to in such a hurry?" Everly demanded, speaking with a more accusatory tone than she'd planned, causing London to whip around.

"What are you doing here?" Eyes wide, London glanced

from side to side, scanning the area to see if they were being observed.

"Relax. Nobody's going to see us." Everly crossed her arms and regarded the younger woman with disdain. "You've been spending a lot of time with Harrison Crosby. Have you been able to get any information out of him that we can use against his brother?"

Everly suspected she already knew the answer, but asked the question anyway. From the way London's gaze shifted away, it was obvious she wasn't taking their revenge pact seriously.

"Look," London quipped, "it's not as if I can just come out and ask Harrison about Tristan's secrets."

"Of course not." Everly reached into her purse and pulled out a USB drive. "That's why I got you this."

London eyed the slim drive for a long second. "What is that?"

"It's a USB drive with a special program on it. You just need to insert it into a port on Tristan's computer, key in a few commands, and it will get you all the information you need off his hard drive."

"Where did you get it?"

"What does it matter?" Everly snapped, her irritation getting away from her. "All you need to know is that it will work."

"How am I supposed to get access to Tristan's computer?"

London was worthless. She was letting her feelings for Harrison distract her from their mission. Fortunately, Everly had thought everything through and had a plan prepared.

"There's a charity polo event coming up at Tristan's plantation," Everly explained. "Make sure you're invited. It will be the perfect opportunity for you to get the information we need."

"That sounds risky."

Everly wanted to shake the other woman. "Do you think you're the only one who's taking chances here?"

"I don't know." London's gaze hardened. "And isn't that the whole point? That we cut off all contact? With each of us handling the other's problems, no one was supposed to be able to trace anything back to us. A onetime meeting at a random event between strangers. Wasn't that the plan? Yet here you are following me from my company. Giving me some sort of technology that I'm supposed to use. What if I get caught and it gets traced back to you?"

"Don't get caught."

London made a disgusted noise. "Can this be traced back to you?"

"No. The person I got it from is very careful."

"Couldn't that person get into Tristan's files? Isn't that what they do?"

"If I wanted to hire the hacker, you'd be unnecessary. And it would be pointless for me to ruin Linc's life on your behalf." Everly neglected to mention the hacker had already tried and failed to access Tristan's laptop remotely as she shoved the USB drive at London. "Just do your part and it will all work out."

Before London could reply, Everly turned on her heel and walked away.

Leave it to a spoiled princess like London McCaffrey

to ruin everything. Of course, she wasn't the only problem. Zoe's progress in taking down Ryan Dailey had stalled, as well. At least Tristan's ex-wife wasn't likely to fall for her target. Crosby had done a number on Zoe during their marriage and subsequent divorce. Chances were Zoe would never trust any man ever again. That worked for Everly. These three men were the worst of the worst and each one of them deserved every terrible thing that would happen to them.

Eight

London spent the days leading up to her dinner with Harrison pondering how she wanted the evening to go. She'd already decided to sleep with him and had prepared her bedroom with freshly washed sheets, flowers and candles for ambience. He probably wouldn't notice any of those touches, but she was an event planner. Arranging the environment to enrich the experience was second nature.

Plus, she didn't want him to catch her off guard a second time. What had happened between them at Upstairs had been amazing, but a little more spontaneous than she was used to. Tonight would be different. She knew what to expect. Could Harrison say the same? Would he realize that she was ready to take things to the next level? After getting her off in a public space, shouldn't he?

By the time he showed up at her door, a bottle of white wine in his hands, she looked poised and pulled together without any sign that she'd spent the weekend cleaning and the last two hours exfoliating head to toe, changing clothes a dozen times, reapplying her makeup twice and generally behaving in a frantic fashion.

"Wow," Harrison said, his sea-glass eyes taking in her appearance.

London had chosen a silky wrap dress in blush pink that flattered her curves and made her feel both sexy and comfortable at the same time. She'd painted her toe-nails a matching pink and left her shoes in her closet, showing the different side of her personality that came out in her own space.

"Thanks," she murmured. "Come on in."

"Did you know that we're neighbors?" he asked, sliding his arm around her waist and bringing her body up against his. "I live in the building next door." He bumped his nose against her neck right below her ear and breathed deeply. "Damn, you smell good."

"Really?" Her toes curled as she draped her arm over his shoulder and tipped her head to give him more access. "I mean about you living next door."

"Crazy, right?" With a sigh, he set her free and brought up the bottle between them. "You said we were having seafood."

"Scallops with risotto."

"Sounds delicious." He accompanied her to the kitchen,

glancing around him as he went. "This is nice. How long have you lived here?"

Her unit faced east, with large floor-to-ceiling windows that overlooked the Cooper River. She'd fallen in love with the condo's hardwood floors and small but high-end kitchen with its white cabinets and marble countertops.

"Three years." She wondered if he'd think the space too neutral. She'd painted the walls a crisp white and paired it with a pale gray sectional, accessorizing with crystal and silver. "How long have you owned your place?"

"Almost five years."

"I'm a little surprised you have a place downtown. You strike me as someone who would prefer a big garage and a lot of outdoor space."

"I've thought about selling, but with my schedule it's easier to live somewhere that I don't have to take care of anything." He was standing at the sliding glass door, looking past her wide terrace and the dark river to the brightly lit Ravenel Bridge. Now he swung around and stepped up to the broad kitchen island. "Need any help?"

She pushed the wine and a corkscrew in his direction. He filled two glasses and brought her one by the stove.

"You cook, too," he said, sounding pleased. "You're a woman of endless talents."

"I like trying out new recipes. I used to entertain a lot, but it's been a while since…" She stopped abruptly, remembering all the dinner parties she and Linc had hosted here.

"You had anyone to cook for?"

She nodded, wishing she hadn't summoned the specter of her ex-fiancé with her careless words. "Maribelle comes over once a week to update me on her wedding plans, but she's worrying about fitting into her dress and so I tend to serve her healthy salads with boiled chicken."

"You can cook for me whenever you want," Harrison said. "Most days during racing season I'm so busy that I live on protein shakes and takeout. Sometimes the racing wives take pity on me and drop by with a home-cooked meal."

"You poor baby," she teased as her phone began to ring.

London noted the caller and winced. She'd been dodging her mother's calls for a week now. Someone had filled Edie in on the new man in her daughter's life and the four voice mails she'd left London had been peppered with her disappointment and unwelcome opinions.

"Do you need to get that?" Harrison asked.

"No."

His eyebrows rose at her hard tone. "Is something wrong?"

"She likes to put her nose where it doesn't belong."

"And where's that?" Harrison leaned his hip against her kitchen island and kept her pinned with his gaze.

"Everything about my life."

"Has she heard you and I are seeing each other?"

"I really don't want to spoil our evening with a conversation about my mother."

"I'll take that as a yes." He sounded unconcerned, but London didn't want him to get the wrong impression.

"I don't care what she thinks. It's none of her business who I see."

"But I'm not the one she'd choose for you."

"It doesn't matter who she'd choose." A defensive edge shaded her tone. "I'm the one dating you."

"I'll bet she was happy you were marrying Linc Thurston."

For what she had planned later, London needed this dinner to be perfect. That wasn't going to happen if a conversation about her mother's elitist attitude ruined the mood.

"If it's okay with you, I really don't want to talk about my mother or my failed engagement."

"I understand."

Something about his somber response warned her he wasn't satisfied with how the conversation had ended.

"I think the risotto is done," she said. "Do you mind bringing the plates over?"

They moved to the dining table and sat down. Candlelight softened Harrison's strong bone structure and gave his sea-glass eyes a mysterious quality as they talked about his race the day before and she updated him on the jazz group she'd booked for his brother's birthday party.

While they ate, London devoured him with her eyes. He was a daredevil. And a competitor. The sort of man who set his eyes on the finish line and went like hell until he got there. Which was why she'd imagined the evening progressing a different way. She'd figured the sexual tension would build during the meal, leading them to fall upon each other before the dessert course.

Instead, Harrison kept the conversation moving from one topic to another. They discussed their parents and favorite vacations growing up. She discovered he hated any drinks with bubbles and she confessed that she was a French fry junkie. It was fun and easy. Yet as they finished the white-chocolate mousse she'd made, and then worked together to fill her dishwasher, London couldn't stop her rising dismay.

Had she made a mistake when she'd assumed they would end up in bed tonight? Harrison seemed as relaxed as she was jumpy. Each brush of his arm against hers had sent her hormones spiraling higher.

Now, as the dishwasher began to hum, she turned to face him. They stared at each other for a long, silent moment. Hunger and anxiety warred within her as she waited for him to make a move. When the tension reached a bursting point, London lifted her hand to the tie that held her dress closed.

It was time to be bold with him. With a single tug, her dress came undone. Harrison remained silent, watching her as she shrugged the material off her shoulders, letting it fall to the floor.

Standing before him in a silk chemise and matching thong, she gave him a sweet smile. "I thought we might watch a movie," she said, toying with a strand of her hair. "Unless you have something else you'd rather do."

He expelled his breath in a half chuckle, one corner

of his mouth kicking up. "We are going to be good together," he declared.

"I know." She twisted a handful of his warm shirt around her knuckles and tugged. "Kiss me."

He obliged, but not in the way she'd hoped. She needed him to claim her mouth and stir her soul. Instead he tormented her by drifting gentle, sweet kisses over her cheeks, eyes, nose and forehead.

"The things I want to do to you," he murmured near her ear.

Relief flooded London even as her breasts ached for his touch. "Like what?"

"Take you into the bedroom." His hand cruised up her side, thumb gliding beneath her breasts, inciting her to arch into his caress with a wordless plea.

If only he'd sweep that thumb over her nipples. Instead he shifted his palm to her back.

"And then?" she prompted, frustration apparent in her voice.

"Strip off your clothes."

Oh...hell...yes. Now they were getting somewhere. "And...then...?"

"Lay you on the bed and spread your gorgeous legs wide open for me."

"Oh..."

His erotic words made her quake. And she suspected that what this man could do to her with his words wouldn't begin to compare to what would happen when his hands and lips met her skin.

"How does that sound?" he asked.

She nodded, excitement momentarily taking away her voice. "What else?" she asked in barely a whisper.

But he'd heard her and smiled. "I'd kiss you everywhere until you were writhing in pleasure."

"Yes, please."

"I'm going to warn you right now," Harrison said. "I'm going to talk during sex."

"What?" Heart thumping madly, London stared at him in helpless delight. "What sort of things are you likely to say?"

"I'll definitely be discussing how beautiful you are and how much you turn me on."

"Do you expect me to answer?" At this point in their relationship London wasn't sure she was ready to crack open her heart and divulge all her thoughts and feelings.

"No expectations. Just relax and listen."

"Relax?" Was he kidding? Already her muscles were tense and nerves twisted in agonized anticipation of his touch. "I feel as if I'll shatter the second you touch me."

"That's not going to happen," he assured her, easing his lips onto hers.

The contact made her sigh. With the release of her breath came a shift in her emotions. Anxiety diminished, replaced by eagerness and undulating waves of pleasure. Instinctively she knew Harrison wouldn't do something that would break her heart. In fact, he might just heal it. If only she could let him.

Except she couldn't.

A giant lie hung between them, casting a shadow over every beautiful emotion that swelled in her chest. Her subterfuge ate at her more and more each day. She longed to be with Harrison even as she recognized that one day her guilt would destroy everything good between them.

Butterflies whirled in her stomach as he grazed his palm up her arm and brushed the strap of her chemise off her shoulder. She pushed all thoughts of the future away as the silk dipped low on her breast. The slide of the soft material tickled her skin and turned up the volume on her eagerness. A tremor shook her as his mouth skated down her neck and into the hollow of her throat. She wanted him. Wanted this. It was simple and at the same time complicated. But mostly it was inevitable.

His fingertips grazed the lace-edged neckline, sweeping the fabric downward. The material momentarily snagged on her sensitized nipple, drawing a sharp gasp from her lips before it fell away, exposing her warm skin to the cool air.

"Your breasts are perfect," he murmured, sliding his lips over their upper curves.

His words sent desire lancing straight to her core. She sank her fingers into his thick curly hair, her throat aching as she held back a cry of protest when his lips glided away from her aching breasts and returned to her shoulder.

With her free hand she slipped the other strap off her shoulder and bared both breasts. "I need your mouth on me. Please, Harrison."

Instead of doing as she'd asked, he leaned back and regarded her expression. Hunger darkened his eyes, strengthening London's desire and bolstering her confidence.

It wasn't as if she was an innocent. She'd known passion, had given herself over to lust and fast, desperate sex.

But what she felt for Harrison wasn't just physical. She genuinely liked him. Appreciated his wry sense of humor, his ability to read her moods and even his fondness for pushing past her boundaries. Deep in her soul she recognized they'd be good together. Better than good. Fantastic.

She and Linc had been together for three years, and with all the time they'd spent apart, she had rarely pictured them making love and grown so horny that she ached for release. Yet almost from the start Harrison had awakened unstoppable cravings. Cravings that on one occasion, all alone in her bed late at night, had compelled her to take matters into her own hands or go half mad.

"Are you wet for me?" He crooned the words, driving her hunger even higher.

"Yes." She gasped the word as his fingers moved between her thighs and grazed across the narrow panel of her thong, sending pleasure lancing through her. She rocked her pelvis in search of more.

"So you are," he purred, stroking her again. "Can you get even wetter?"

"Keep that up—" Her voice broke as he applied light pressure to the knot of nerves between her thighs. A blissful shudder left her panting. "And see."

He gave a husky little laugh.

"What if I bury my face between your thighs and taste you?"

Her legs had been on the verge of giving out before his offer. Now yearning battered her, making her achy and needy. But mostly it made her impatient.

"Harrison," she blurted out.

Every part of her was shaking. Her knees were threatening to buckle. But instinctively she knew he'd take care of her. She wouldn't crumple to the ground. He'd be there to lift her and carry her into pleasure unlike anything she'd ever known.

"Yes, London?"

His clever fingers slipped beneath the elastic of her panties and stroked her so perfectly she thought she might die from it. She clenched her eyes shut and struggled to draw enough breath into her lungs to tell him what she wanted.

"I don't want our first time to be here," she said, though she was on the verge of not caring that she'd spent hours setting the stage for a perfect evening. "Take me," she gasped with what air his skillful touch hadn't stolen from her, "to the bedroom."

Harrison didn't care where their first time was as long as she was happy.

Without a word, he bent down and lifted her into his arms. She gave up a joyous laugh as she roped her arms around his neck and dropped soft kisses along his jawline while directing him down a hallway.

Her bedroom was like the rest of the condo. Cool and refined with a few decadent touches like a fuzzy throw rug, a vase of pink roses on the dresser to scent the air and a dozen flickering candles casting wavering light over the gray walls.

She'd planned this, he realized. Invited him for dinner with the purpose of sleeping with him. What a woman.

He set her on her feet inside the door and pulled her into his arms for a long, sexy kiss. Electricity jolted through him as she drove her tongue into his mouth and let him taste her desire. Rich and vibrant, the kiss promised fantasies he hadn't yet dreamed up.

Tonight was about finding out more about London. And something told him she was going to surprise him.

"I'm obsessed with your mouth," she said when he broke off the kiss and set his forehead against hers. Trembling fingers skimmed over his lips. "I can't stop thinking about all the places I want you to kiss me."

He answered her with a smile, letting his eyes speak for him. Gaze locked on his lips, she sighed.

"I've tried to fight this," she continued. "Tried to remain sensible, but just hearing your voice gets me hot."

Harrison smoothed his palms along her spine and across her hips. He didn't want to say or do anything that would stop this confession. She made him feel things he'd never known and it was heaven to hear her echoing his own needs and desires.

"How hot?"

"My skin burns. My nipples ache. I want you to take them in your mouth and suck hard."

His groan was ragged and rough. "Keep going." The command was nearly incoherent as he set his lips against her shoulder.

She looped her arms around his shoulders and tipped her head, baring her long, white neck to his determined seduction. Taking advantage of what she offered, he lowered his lips to her skin and brought both tongue and teeth into play. Her muscles jerked as he nipped and a low moan rumbled up from her chest.

"Oh, Harrison." Her husky voice hitched, betraying how turned on she was, and despite the almost painful ache below his belt, he grinned.

He backed her toward the bed, divesting himself of shirt and shoes as he went. Hooking his fingers into her thong, he pulled the bit of silk and lace off her hips and down her thighs. She shivered as he knelt at her feet and helped her step out of the fabric.

While she scooted onto the bed, he stripped off his pants and underwear. As soon as it was free, his erection pointed straight at her. London reclined on the mattress, propping herself up on her elbows, her eyes gobbling him up.

Seeing that she had his full attention, she let her knees fall apart, opening herself to him. The sight of her so pink and wet and perfect made Harrison want to shout in jubilation. Grinning, he prowled onto the mattress.

"You are beautiful." He trailed his fingers across her skin, lingering over her neat strip of hair that led straight to where he longed to go. "Especially here."

"Really?" She stared at herself and frowned.

"You can't appreciate it the way I can." He grazed his finger through her slick folds and her eyes popped open as a throaty cry burst from her lips. "I love how you're so sensitive."

"You bring that out in me," she murmured, her words coming in soft pants.

Grinning, he lowered his face between her legs and stroked his tongue through her heat. Her hips bucked while a sharp curse escaped her.

"Warn a girl," she gasped, pressing toward his mouth.

His breath puffed out in a chuckle. "I'm going to put my mouth on you and drive you crazy before I let you come."

"Better." She moaned as he went back for a second taste.

Her scent and sweetness made him smile as he devoured her. Each movement of his tongue caused her to moan. Her fingers dived into his hair, digging into his scalp as he drew her pulsing clit between his lips and gently sucked. She gave a half shriek before calling his name. Her hips twisted as she took her pleasure against his mouth.

"Oh, Harrison," she cried, her voice raspy and broken. "That's so good."

He gathered her butt in his palms and opened his eyes to watch her every response as he continued to ply her with lips and tongue. As in everything she did, her body moved with perfect grace. Yet her usual reserve had vanished. She was completely caught up in the moment, her hips rotating like she was dancing for him. It was so incredibly sensual that he just knew he had to push her pleasure still higher.

Harrison redoubled his effort, plying her with every trick he knew. She wouldn't know what hit her when she climaxed. But first, he had to make sure she was thoroughly familiar with the joys he could bring her.

"Harrison, it's too…" She grabbed a handful of the quilt and pulled hard enough to cause her knuckles to go white.

"Touch your breasts," he commanded, wondering if she was too far gone to hear him. "Show me how I make you feel."

To his shock, she released his hair and the quilt and gathered her beautiful breasts into her hands, kneading and rolling her nipples through her fingers, displaying an abandon he never imagined he'd see.

"Oh," she groaned. "More. More. Yes."

Her impassioned cries made him harder than he'd ever been before. But this moment wasn't for him. At least not directly. He took great satisfaction in driving her wild. Recognizing how badly she wanted to come, he slid two fingers inside her. Her head came off the bed and an incoherent noise tore from her throat.

"That's it, baby. Give me all you've got." He squeezed her butt cheeks and drove his mouth hard against her clit, grinning as her body began to shudder. "Let go."

"It's…it's…incredible," she exclaimed and then, with one long keening cry, started to come apart.

Harrison watched it all unfold. There was nothing so perfect in the whole world as London McCaffrey so aroused she became utterly lost in her pleasure, rocking and arching as she drove herself against his mouth.

A powerful orgasm moved through her and he savored each wave as it battered her.

When her body grew limp, he eased his mouth off her and tracked butterfly kisses across her pelvis and over her abdomen. Her chest heaved as she labored to recover her breath. She lay with her hands plastered over her eyes as a series of incoherent noises tumbled from her lips.

"You okay?" he asked, gliding his lips up her body and noting the glorious glow her skin had taken on in the wake of her climax.

"What did you do to me?" she mumbled, sounding shaken and utterly spent.

"I'm pretty sure I gave you an orgasm." He made no attempt to hide his smugness and hoped she wasn't feeling overly sensitive about how she'd let go. It had been sexy as hell and he didn't want her to retreat from him. "A big one."

She spread her fingers and peered at him. "What am I going to do with you?"

A second later she answered her own question by dropping her hand to his erection, making him moan. "Just give that a stroke or two." His voice became a croak as she followed his instructions, demonstrating that she was eager to please him in kind. "No need to be gentle. It's not going to break."

"Like that?"

A series of provocative strokes made him groan. "That works."

He bent and kissed her deep, showing her how much he liked having her hand on him.

"This is nice," she murmured when they broke apart. "But it would be better if you'd slide on a condom and make love to me."

He didn't need to be asked twice. In seconds he'd located the foil packet and rolled on protection. She watched his actions through half-lidded eyes, lower lip trapped between her teeth. He paused a second to appreciate her tousled blond hair and passion-bruised lips. Then sliding between her thighs, he guided himself to her tight entrance, the tip dipping in, testing her acceptance. The feel of her, so open and receptive, made him want the moment to be perfect for her.

Brushing a strand of hair off her flushed cheek, he kissed her softly. "You ready?"

"Do you really have to ask?"

It took all his concentration to take it slow and let her adjust to him. What he hadn't considered was his equal need to adjust to her. Her breath shuddered out in a long, slow exhalation as he filled her. It was as if she'd liberated something she'd been holding on to for a long time.

As the long, slow thrust came to an end, she opened her eyes and met his gaze. The trust he glimpsed there made him feel like the most powerful man alive.

"Babe, you feel incredible," he murmured, making good on his promise to talk. "So tight and hot. I love the way your muscles grab me. Like you want me there."

"I do." Her palms coasted down his back and over his butt. She gripped him with surprising strength, fingers digging into his muscles, pulling him hard against her. "I love having you inside me."

"It's not too much?"

She shook her head. "I think we're a perfect fit."

"So do I."

And then there was no further need for words. It was a blend of hands, lips, tongue, breath and skin as they rocked together, discovering each other on a whole new level. To say being inside her felt good was a massive understatement. She was all heat and hunger and intensity as she wrapped her legs around his waist and clung to him.

He thrust into her, finding a steady, pounding rhythm she seemed to like. Her hips moved in time with his, matching his intensity and even taking the wildness up a notch.

"Harrison, please," she begged, inner muscles clamping down on him. "Make me come again. Now. I need you."

Harrison had never been one to disappoint a lady. He slid his palm beneath her, lifting her off the mattress. Gripping her firmly, he went to work, watching her beautiful face for every nuance, adjusting his thrusts to bump her clit each time he plunged into her. And plunge he did. Over and over, gritting his teeth, a growl burning in his throat as he held back his own pleasure.

And then her back arched and a strained cry erupted from her lips. She drove her nails into his shoulder and summoned his name from some endless depth. Her body bucked against his, driving into his thrusts. Seconds later she was shuddering in a long series of ripples that drew him right over the edge after her.

With a final thrust, he collapsed onto his forearms, head falling to the mattress above her shoulder. She shifted so their sweaty cheeks pressed together. His chest heaved as he labored to draw breath into his lungs. It took effort for him to open his eyes. More still to lift his head. But he needed to look into her eyes to see for himself that the world-stopping sex had been just as amazing for her.

To his dismay, her eyes were closed. She was equally winded, but her features were relaxed into an expression of satisfaction.

"London?"

"That was way better than I expected." Her eyes flashed open. A possessive look blazed there for a moment before she let her lashes fall. "And I expected a lot."

He levered himself to one side, coming to rest beside her, his head propped on his hand. A strand of hair clung to her forehead. He brushed it off, delighting in the quiet moment. She lifted her hand and cupped his cheek. Her thumb grazed over his lower lip.

"Now I'm not just obsessed with your mouth," she said, sounding drowsy, "but with your dick, as well."

Harrison's jaw dropped. Had she really just said that? Did her society friends have any idea this woman existed? He didn't think so. In fact, if he had to guess, he'd say that London hadn't realized the depth of her wantonness until recently.

"It's happy to hear that," he murmured, sliding his arms around her and pulling her firmly against his body. "And so am I."

Nine

With her left hand firmly clasped in Harrison's right, London's heart picked up speed as he angled the Mercedes onto the driveway and streaked through the Crosby Motorsports entrance gate. Above them, the company logo flanked by the four Crosby team car numbers welcomed employees and fans alike.

London had been silent through most of the thirty-minute car ride, content to listen to Harrison narrate the history of his uncle's rise to being number three on the all-time winner's cup victories list for the racing league. And number two in modern-day wins. His teams had won at least one championship-level race each season since 2000 and Jack had ten owner's championships.

Tonight they were heading to an end-of-the-season party for the six hundred employees who'd assisted

Crosby Motorsports in achieving its third-place cup finish. It was London's first official appearance as Harrison's girlfriend and all day she'd been queasy as she grappled with the potential repercussions of how far she'd let things go.

The flash drive Everly had given her was a psychological burden bearing down on her heart. Each day she didn't use it was another day she hadn't betrayed Harrison. The woman who'd agreed to take revenge on Tristan was someone she no longer identified with. And what did she really owe Everly and Zoe?

Fifteen buildings made up the four-hundred thousand-square-foot state-of-the-art facility that supported four full-time Ford teams. Walking hand in hand, London and Harrison neared the company's heritage center. The site of the original race shop when the company was founded in 1990, the building housed Jack Crosby's extensive car collection.

The flow of guests swept them into the building and past several exhibits, which Harrison explained were popular fan destinations. Freestanding bars had been placed in strategic locations so the guests could get a drink ahead of the dinner being served in a giant tent erected outside.

"Some night I'll bring you back here and give you a proper tour," he promised as they strolled hand in hand past rare cars.

"What's wrong with now?" she asked him.

"I misspoke. I meant an improper tour. Have you ever wanted to make out in the back of a rare 1969 Chevy

Camaro?" He hooked a thumb at the bright orange car beside them.

She shot him a droll look even as her cheeks heated. "Do I seem the sort of girl who'd ever have that sort of fantasy?"

Even as she spoke, however, the place between her thighs tingled. She imagined herself grinding on him in one of these vehicles, steaming up the windows and watching his face as he came. What was he doing to her? London shivered in pleasure while his fingers pulsed against hers as if he'd read her mind.

"I suspect you've already done things with me you never imagined."

He wasn't wrong and she gave a little shrug. Before she could figure out what to say, however, a young man approached them asking if Harrison would come meet his grandmother. She was a huge fan and hampered by arthritic knees.

"Go ahead," London said. "I'm going to find the ladies' room."

"Meet you back here?" He glanced toward the Camaro. "You can consider my offer while I'm gone."

"I'll be waiting," she replied.

Ten minutes later she returned to the spot to await Harrison, unsurprised that he hadn't made it back. From what she'd seen of him at the track and when they'd encountered his fans out and about, he was always happy to sign autographs and take photos.

The blend of adrenaline junkie, focused athlete and all-around good guy had slipped through London's defenses. His daring and honed reflexes were remarkably sexy, yet the fact that every second behind the wheel could result in disaster somehow made Harrison relaxed and calm.

His composure was a complete contrast to the emotional minefield London found herself in. Happiness. Guilt. Responsibility. Selfishness. She wanted to bask in the joy of her growing connection with Harrison, but worry and obligation tormented her. Allowing herself to blissfully date Harrison while Zoe waited in limbo for Tristan to suffer couldn't last much longer. Time was nearly up. She had to act even if that meant she would be compelled to end things with Harrison.

As if summoned by her thoughts, Tristan appeared in her line of sight. He strolled through the swarm of people as if he was the most important person in the room. He didn't radiate confidence as much as blare it. Several women and some men followed his progress and London couldn't blame them. The perfection of his strong, chiseled features, styled hair and powerful build made it hard to remain immune.

In his elegant charcoal suit, he looked broadershouldered than Harrison, although she suspected his bulk wasn't all muscle. London knew firsthand the strength in Harrison's lean body. He was honed and sculpted by hours of mental and physical training.

Tristan looked less like a hungry cheetah and more like a sated lion. Either way he was dangerous. Which was why she felt that she'd been punched in the solar plexus when he caught her staring at him. Almost immediately he shifted direction and made a beeline for her. Cursing her lack of subtlety, she slapped a pleasant expression on her face as he neared.

"We meet again," Tristan said as he entered her space, eyeing her with an interest he hadn't shown during their first encounter. He held out his hand. "London, isn't it?"

"Yes." She gave him her hand and resisted the urge to yank it away as his fingers slid over hers in a way that was overly familiar. "I'm surprised you remembered me. We met so briefly at your aunt's charity function."

"You're a stunning woman." There was no mistaking the sensual glow in his eyes. "I remember thinking I'd like to get to know you better."

She doubted that. He'd barely given her the time of day before moving on to a woman with an impressive cleavage. So why the sudden interest now?

Confusion reigned as she forced a polite smile. "I'm flattered."

"You don't look as if you belong here any more than I do," Tristan said, echoing what would've been London's opinion a few short weeks earlier.

She glanced away from him and surveyed the party guests, noting the difference from the charity event where she'd first met Harrison and his brother. That evening the women had been dressed in expensive gowns and dripping with jewels. They'd navigated the room dispensing sugary phrases in droll tones.

Tonight's assembly wore jeans, team apparel and the occasional blazer or party dress. London recognized that she stood out in the leopard pumps she'd borrowed from Maribelle and her classic little black dress. As when she'd gone to the racetrack in Richmond, her styling choices highlighted that she didn't have much in common with these unpretentious people. No wonder Tristan had approached her. He wore a gorgeous custom suit in dark gray more appropriate to the yacht club than a tent.

"I have to admit this isn't exactly my regular crowd," London said, hating the way that sounded even though it was true. "I take it you don't have much to do with Crosby Motorsports?"

"Hardly." Tristan glanced around before leaning down as if to share a confidence with her. "My brother is the one who likes to get his hands dirty." His sneer made his contempt for Harrison clear and the contrast between the brothers grew starker. "The fact that he races cars has made him an embarrassment to our family."

London wondered if Tristan had any idea she and Harrison had been seeing each other. "He's quite successful at it."

"Successful…" Once again his gaze moved over her, this time lingering at her neckline. "Don't tell me you're one of those racing groupies. You appear to have a little too much class for that."

The man's prejudice was so blatant that London found herself momentarily speechless. And as she grappled with a response, it occurred to her that she'd been equally snobbish in the beginning, before she'd gotten to know Harrison. Shame brought heat to her cheeks.

"Feel like getting out of here?" Tristan's fingers curved over her hip, lingering for a few seconds as if to test her reaction. When shock kept her from pulling away, he must've taken that as encouragement because his palm slid over her backside and he gave her butt a suggestive squeeze. "My house is twenty minutes away."

London thought about the flash drive she'd taken to carrying in her purse. What excuse could she give Harrison that would let her slip away with Tristan and get the information off his computer? Her mind spun as she conceived and discarded a dozen justifications for leaving the party with Tristan. None of them made any sense.

"I—"

She never got to finish her refusal because Harrison emerged from the crowd and spied her standing with his brother. His brows came together in a frown that was half annoyance and half confusion as he noticed where Tristan's hand had gone. With an inaudible gasp, London stepped away from Tristan and tried to catch Harrison's gaze as he approached them, but his attention was firmly fixed on his brother.

"What are you doing here?" Harrison demanded, his expression and tone unfriendly.

"I am the head of Crosby Automotive."

"That doesn't answer my question."

"This is a family business," Tristan pointed out.

"And you've made it pretty clear you want nothing to do with us." Harrison's eyes narrowed. "Or at least that's been your attitude before your profits started to dip. What? Are you hoping to convince Jack to help you out financially?"

Tristan's expression darkened. He obviously didn't

appreciate his younger brother pointing out his short-comings.

"I don't need his help or yours," Tristan said. "And this little shindig of yours is a complete bore. I've got better things to do." With an elaborate sigh, he glanced at London and gestured toward the door. "Shall we?"

Harrison turned stunned eyes her way and London opened her mouth to explain, but her scrambled brain produced no words. Why hadn't she come straight out and told Tristan she was dating Harrison? Scheming was not her forte.

"She's not going anywhere with you," Harrison said.

"Why don't you let the lady decide?"

"Ah, actually I came here with Harrison," London said, cringing as she realized it was too little, too late.

She now understood that balancing her growing affection for Harrison against taking down his brother wasn't possible. It was either one or the other and the moment for her to choose was now.

"You two are dating?" Tristan asked, laughter in his voice.

"Well…" she hedged.

Harrison suffered none of her hesitation. "Yes."

While Tristan laughed at their diverging answers, London stared at Harrison. She found herself short of breath as their gazes clashed. In his sea-glass eyes she saw her future. The beauty of it struck her and suddenly she wanted to cry. She'd ruined everything.

"Sounds like you two need to sort out what's going on." Tristan squeezed London's arm. "If you get tired of slumming, give me a call."

She remained silent, biting the inside of her lip as Harrison's brother walked away. Words gathered in her throat but a lump prevented them from escaping. On the heels of the realization that she'd let the encounter with Tristan get away from her came the recognition that by falling for Harrison, she'd put her emotions in direct conflict with her promise to help Zoe.

"I thought we were on the same page," Harrison said. "If we're not dating, then what are we doing?"

"I don't know." As much as she wanted to escape his questions, he deserved honesty and openness. "This wasn't supposed to get complicated."

He frowned. "Because I'm not the man you think you want?"

"What?"

She was starting to believe he was the only man for her. And she'd made a mess of things.

His eyes flicked in the direction his brother had departed. "Are you thinking he could make you happy? Because he is incapable of putting anyone's feelings above his own."

"I'm not interested in your brother." At least not in the way Harrison was insinuating. How could she defuse this argument without committing herself one way or another? "In fact, I was in the process of defending you when he hit on me. You interrupted us before I could react."

Harrison assessed her for a long moment and whatever he glimpsed in her expression caused him to relax. "I don't need you to defend me."

"I know." Yet she could see he appreciated it. She

took his hand in both of hers and stepped into his space, waiting until the tension seeped from his body before she finished. "But there was no way I was going to stand by and let him criticize what you do."

"It seems to me that you felt the same a couple weeks ago." He snaked his arm around her waist and pulled her tight against him.

"All the more reason for me to have your back. I was ignorant and shortsighted. You're doing what you love and no one has the right to judge you for it. Not even your brother."

"Fine. I forgive you," he said, cupping her cheek while his lips dropped to hers.

His kiss was romantic and intoxicating. She threw herself into the embrace, shoving her worries aside for the moment. Later she would delve into the ever-deepening mess she was making of things.

How long they stood in the middle of the crowded party, lost in each other, London had no idea. But when Harrison eventually set her free, London returned to her body with a jolt.

What magic drove all thoughts of propriety and decorum from her mind whenever he took her in his arms? She'd never acted like this before and loved every second of it.

By contrast, her relationship with Linc had always been so proper. She'd certainly never thrown her arms around his neck and kissed him with utter abandon in a public place. She'd always been hyperaware of how things looked and who might be watching. With Harrison, even though he was also a celebrity, she never considered appearances before showing affection with him.

"I'm sorry," she murmured when he ended the kiss.

"For what?"

So many things. "The way I feel when I'm with you is thrilling and scary all at once and way more intense than anything I've known before."

He kissed her forehead. "For me it's the exact opposite. Being with you calms me down. When we're together, it feels right."

Tears burned London's eyes. The man was just too perfect and she didn't deserve the happiness he brought her. Dabbing at the corner of her eye in what she hoped was a surreptitious manner, London took his hand in hers and exhaled heartily.

"You always say the right thing," she told him, wishing he'd demonstrate some of his brother's villainy. It would make using him to her advantage easier to swallow.

"Ready to go find our table?"

"Lead the way."

"This is quite a place," London remarked, taking in the state-of-the-art barn, paddocks, polo field and sprawling home with views that overlooked the horse pastures all belonging to Harrison's brother.

She'd started scoping out the house as soon as it had come into view, needing to find a way in so she could use the USB drive in her purse. The task terrified her. What if she was caught? Or the drive didn't work? Or the information they needed wasn't on his computer. So much could go wrong.

As Everly promised, Harrison had invited her to the charity polo event hosted at Tristan's property outside Charleston. She'd attended functions like this often with Linc. He'd loved giving back to the community. In fact, this particular charity was a pet project of his.

No doubt she could look forward to running into her ex. Would he be surprised that she was here with Harrison? Given what she'd heard about his relationship with his housekeeper, would he even care?

"I can't imagine how much it costs to maintain all this," she continued, anxiety making her remarks clumsy. "And he has a house in the historic district, as well? Crosby Automotive must be doing really well."

Harrison gave her an odd look.

Was she being too obvious in her interest again? "It's quite a bit of real estate," she added nervously.

"I guess. I've never really thought about it."

"And all these horses, it must cost a fortune to maintain them."

"Look, you really suck at beating around the bush," Harrison said, his tone slightly aggrieved. "Is there something you want to ask?"

"I'm being nosy, but I heard that his ex-wife ended up with next to nothing in the divorce settlement because Tristan wasn't doing all that well financially."

Harrison shrugged. "That might be what she's telling people. But what she got in the divorce might have more to do with something that triggered certain clauses in her prenuptial agreement."

"Oh."

London already knew what Harrison was referring to. Zoe had been accused of infidelity, a charge Tristan trumped up. There had been photos and hotel room charges. She'd disputed the accusation and proved her innocence, but the fight had racked up legal fees, eating up her small settlement. Meanwhile Tristan had cheated on her to his heart's content with no repercussions.

"You don't believe that?" Harrison asked, his ability to read her proving troublesome once again.

"I guess that makes sense."

All too aware she'd really put her foot in it, London cast around for a distraction and spied Everly in the crowd. Every encounter with the woman had driven London's anxiety higher and she tensed. Beside her, ever sensitive to her reactions, Harrison sent his palm skating up her spine in a soothing caress.

"Something wrong?" he asked, regarding her with concern in his sea-glass eyes.

What excuse could she give him? London's brain scrambled for anything that sounded reasonable but came up empty. At her lack of response, his gaze swept the crowd. Not far from Everly, Linc and his sister were strolling side by side through the crowd. He looked happy. Moving on had obviously been good for him.

In contrast, London's nerves were twisted into knots and her stomach felt as if she were on a small boat tossed by stormy seas. In the month since she and Harrison had first gone to dinner, the pain of her broken engagement had faded to a distant memory. She had Harrison to thank for that. Since that night at her condo, they'd been together almost every night. Sometimes at her place. Sometimes at his. Occasionally she wondered at her lack of interest in going out to dinner or in joining Maribelle and Beau for drinks. Having Harrison all to herself was addictive and she'd noticed herself almost constantly basking in the warm glow of contentment that he was in her life.

"Ah," Harrison said, bringing her back to the present. He'd noticed Linc and assumed that was why she was acting so strange. "Are you going to be okay?"

"Sure. Fine." London shook her head. "It's all good."

"Are you sure?"

Although he sounded concerned, his expression had gone flat. He'd obviously misinterpreted the reason for her dismay. London imagined how she'd feel if Harrison had an ex-fiancée and she was attending the same party. Not that Harrison could ever be described as insecure.

"Of course." London gave the declaration an extra punch to reassure him all was well. "It's water under the bridge."

"Is that why you're so tense?"

Damn the man for being so perceptive. London noticed her shoulders had started climbing toward her ears and made an effort to relax them. Usually only her mother had such a strong effect on her, but London had to admit Everly Briggs scared her.

"I haven't seen him since our engagement ended," London said. "It just takes a little getting used to." Pleasure suffused her at the concern in Harrison's eyes. As accustomed as she was to being strong all the time, it was a welcome change to lean on someone else. "Thank you for worrying about me."

And then, because actions spoke louder than words, she grabbed a handful of Harrison's bright blue blazer. Throwing propriety to the wind, she tugged him to her. Her high heels put her lips within kissing distance of his and Harrison obliged her by dipping his head. The kiss electrified her, sensation racing through her body with familiar and joyful results. She grew light-headed almost immediately and was glad for the strong arm he wrapped around her waist.

Thanks to him the kiss didn't spin out of control. If left up to her, London would have tugged him into a private corner and let her fingers find their way beneath his crisp white dress shirt. As it was, they were both breathing a little unsteadily when he lifted his head.

"Damn," he murmured in wonder. "You do surprise me sometimes."

"That's good, right?"

"Absolutely." He dropped a light kiss on her nose and relaxed his arm, letting her draw a deep breath. "Let's go claim some seats."

They found a spot near the center of the field and sat. Harrison hadn't relinquished her hand and London found herself having a difficult time concentrating on the match as he toyed with her fingers. It made her thoughts return to the morning and revisit how his caresses had danced over her skin until she'd begged him for release.

Her musings were interrupted by another glimpse of Everly. To London's dismay, the woman caught her eye and frowned at her. After she'd made her displeasure known, Everly glanced significantly in Linc's direction. London's ex-fiancé was chatting with several of his friends, but his attention was obviously not on the conversation. He was watching a slender brunette set up the picnic baskets for lunch.

London recognized Claire Robbins, Linc's housekeeper. All the gossip and speculation circulating about those two coalesced into reality and London felt... nothing. No regret. No jealousy. No shame. It was as if she'd gotten over Linc. Or she'd realized there wasn't anything to get over and that he'd been right to end their engagement.

Smiling, she glanced Harrison's way, but saw that his attention was on the polo match. As much as she wanted to share her epiphany with him, she kept silent. Everly's presence at the event reminded London that she had an ulterior motive for being here today.

The need to get into Tristan's house and plug the USB drive into his computer preoccupied London through the second match of the day and into the lunch break. The picnic-basket lunches for two that had been created by Claire were a delightful surprise to London. She had no idea how Linc's housekeeper had come to cater such a function or that she'd had any culinary leanings. The food was fantastic. There'd been a sandwich sampler made with beef, ham and salmon. The basket also contained an artisanal meat-and-cheese tray with a fabulous kale salad, fresh fruit, a bottle of Txakoli, and homemade aguas frescas made from melons, strawberry and mango. London did little more than sample everything, but the sheer volume of food left her feeling thoroughly stuffed and a bit sleepy.

"That was amazing," she murmured, settling back in her chair with a groan.

"There's still dessert." Harrison gestured toward the food tent and the tables filled with trays of triple-layer chocolate cake, mini cheesecakes, tiny tortes, mousse and chocolate-covered strawberries.

"I couldn't possibly," London said, deciding this might be the opening she'd been looking for. "You go ahead. I'm going to take a quick walk and find a ladies' room."

With all the people milling around, it was surprisingly easy to gain entrance into Tristan's home. She was almost disappointed that the doors weren't locked because then she'd have a perfect excuse to turn around. What if someone caught her sneaking in? London lifted her chin and settled her nerves with a calming breath. The best thing to do would be to get it over with as quickly as possible.

It took her less than five minutes to locate Tristan's study. Heart pounding, London moved into the room and eased the door shut behind her. If she was caught in here, she had no explanation for sitting at his desk and perusing his laptop computer. This was madness. Was any of this worth the damage to her relationship with Harrison?

The question shocked London to her toes and made her chest ache. She craved more time with Harrison. More hours of conversation. More minutes holding his hand. More mornings sharing breakfast with him. More nights making love. More weeks to let their intimate

connection grow and flourish. More years to build a
life with him.

All of it was a foolish fantasy. There was no future
with Harrison. The fact that she was standing in his
brother's study on the verge of stealing the contents
of Tristan's computer established where she'd placed
her loyalty.

Fighting a sudden rush of helplessness, London
pressed her back against the wall, letting her gaze roam
the space. It was a typical masculine study with two
of the walls lined in dark paneling, the others sporting
hunting scenes and bookshelves. Heavy hunter green
drapes framed the single window. An expensive Ori-
ental rug stretched from her toes to a large, ornately
carved wooden desk.

Move.

The longer she stayed in place, questioning her judgment, the more likely she was to get caught. Barely
discernible above the thundering of her heart came the
cheers from the crowd watching the polo match outside.
She didn't have a lot of time. If she was gone too long,
Harrison would start to wonder what was keeping her.

Tiptoeing across the rug to Tristan's desk seemed a
bit ridiculous, but since London was breaking into the
man's computer, she might as well act like a thief. Her
hands shook as she rounded the enormous mahogany
desk and approached his computer. She opened the laptop
and the screen came to life. Unsurprisingly, the desktop
displayed an image of Tristan on one of his polo ponies,
looking suave and ruggedly masculine as he stared down
the photographer.

Shivering with foreboding, London quickly found where to plug in the drive but hesitated before inserting it into the slot. Her heart raced, keeping pace with the rumble of hoof beats on the polo grounds. If she was going to do this, it needed to be now. Yet she continued to flounder.

And then the sound of approaching voices reached her: a woman's high-pitched laughter followed by a man's deep baritone. London jerked away from the computer, bumping into the desk chair and sending it thumping back against the wall. The noise seemed to explode in the quiet room and she glanced around wildly, looking for a place to hide before the couple entered. The long drapes caught her eye. In seconds she slipped behind the voluminous fabric, hoping she was out of sight.

Pulse jumping erratically, she waited. And waited. Expecting the door to open at any second, she tried to calm her rapid breathing but alarm had her firmly in its grasp. Had it been Tristan in the hallway? London recalled their encounter at the Crosby Motorsports end-of-season party. No doubt he had a string of women he entertained. The man's insatiable appetites weren't just gossip. He'd cheated on Zoe almost from the beginning of their marriage.

London wasn't sure how much time she spent behind the curtain before she realized no one was coming into the study. She eased out and glanced at the desk before making her way to the door. After straining to hear if anyone occupied the hall, she gathered a bracing breath and opened the door a crack. There was no one around, so she slipped out of Tristan's study and made her way back outside. Not until she reached sunlight and fresh air did she take a full breath. A second later the air whooshed out of her lungs in a squeak as someone spoke.

"Did you do it?"

London whirled around and spied Everly standing beside the side door. Her eyes gleamed with feral intensity.

"I couldn't."

"The program didn't work?"

London gripped the flash drive tighter. Would she have gone through with it if not for the near interruption? It was a question she'd be asking herself for a long time. How far was she planning to go to hurt someone she didn't know just to take revenge on Linc for ending their engagement? Especially when she no longer felt hurt and betrayed.

When she, Everly and Zoe had first concocted the plan, London had been reeling from the shock and hurt, and was feeling vengeful. But since Harrison had come along, she'd realized that Linc wasn't the only man in the world for her. Maybe he never was.

"I didn't try it," London admitted.

"Why not?"

"I'm not sure we're doing the right thing."

"Why? Because you're dating Harrison? Suddenly it's okay for you to back out on our agreement because you're happy? Is that fair to Zoe? She's living in the back room of the boutique she opened and can't pay her rent because the divorce lawyer got all her savings."

Because they weren't supposed to be in contact with each other, London hadn't had any idea Zoe's situation was so dire. "I'll give her some money to get by."

Everly ejected an exasperated snort. "You can't help her like that. The point of what we're doing is to not have any contact with each other."

"And yet you're here talking to me," London pointed out, glancing around and seeing that they were completely alone. "And apparently you've been keeping tabs on Zoe to know her current situation."

"I'm doing my part," Everly said, not responding to London's accusation. "If you don't do yours, then Zoe has no reason to go after Ryan. That man destroyed my sister and I intend to make him pay."

"I don't know," London hedged, unnerved by Everly's savagery. "This is all just so much more than I signed on for."

"Listen up," Everly said, leaning close, her manner intimidating. "We made a deal and you're going to see it through."

"Deals can be broken."

Abruptly, Everly's demeanor changed and she became cool and collected once again. "I wondered if this might happen with you. This is one deal you're not going to break."

"What are you going to do to stop me?" London asked, sounding more confident than she felt.

Everly's quicksilver mood change intensified London's concerns. What sort of unbalanced person had she gotten mixed up with?

"I've set things in motion that are going to ruin Linc's

life. That was what I promised I would do. You need to do your part. You owe me and you owe Zoe."

"I'm out." London started to slide past Everly. To her surprise, the other woman grabbed her arm in a tight vise. "Let me go."

"If you don't go through with this, I will reveal to Harrison what you've been up to."

Panic flooded her and London scrambled for what to say to defuse the situation. The only way she knew to limit Everly's blackmail potential was to deny her feelings for Harrison.

"You'll only blow up this whole scheme if you do. I've used Harrison to get to Tristan. He means nothing to me except as a means to an end. If you tell him what I've been up to, we all go down."

That said, she yanked her arm from Everly's grasp, feeling the rake of the woman's nails against her skin as she pulled free. It wasn't in London to shove the woman before escaping, but if anyone deserved to be knocked around in that moment, it was Everly.

London walked away as swiftly as she dared, conscious that she'd already been away from Harrison for too long. Heat surged beneath her skin as her heart and lungs pumped adrenaline through her whole body. She couldn't go back to Harrison in this emotionally heightened state. He would want to know what was wrong. What could she tell him?

And then her gaze fell on a small group and the one individual who was utterly familiar to her. Lincoln faced Claire Robbins, and from her devastated expression and the anguish on his face, London realized whatever Everly had set in motion between Linc and the woman he loved had just come to a head.

Grief and rage hit her already raw nerves and London sped away from the crowds as her stomach pitched sickeningly. What had they done? What had she done? Linc didn't deserve to have his life ruined because he'd broken off their engagement. He'd been right that they didn't belong together. Only she'd been too busy wallowing in what she'd perceived as her failure to see it.

Tears blinded her as bile filled her mouth and anguish twisted her heart. She was well and truly stuck now that Everly had exacted London's revenge on Linc. Her chance to escape the situation long gone.

London made her way toward the refreshment tent where the lunches had been available earlier. She needed some water and a quiet moment to herself. What a fool she'd been to make such a terrible pact. Her fingers tightened over the flash drive. The moment to use it was gone. And London was relieved.

Everly's threat filled her mind. London had no doubt that Everly would tell Harrison what was going on even if it meant ruining everything for all of them. The woman was crazy. Or maybe it was London who'd lost it. She was still trying to figure out how she could get the incriminating information on Tristan and not let her actions destroy what she was building with Harrison. Talk about being stuck between a rock and a hard place.

Harrison had finished a full plate of desserts without London reappearing and wondered where she'd gotten herself off to.

The day had started out cloudless and warm for late November. Harrison's optimism had been sky-high. He'd considered their first appearance in Charleston society as a couple to be a statement about their relationship.

It had been.

Just not in the way he'd expected.

Ever since London had spied Linc Thurston, Harrison had noticed a nagging disquiet. No, that wasn't quite true. He'd been troubled since the first night he and London had slept together after she admitted her mother didn't believe Harrison was the sort of man London should date.

Normally he didn't care about anyone's opinions, but the closer he and London grew, the more he wondered when her mother would put pressure on her to find someone more suitable. Harrison had no idea if she'd fight for them or cave to her mother's will and that bothered him a lot.

Harrison had assumed he'd come to know London quite well during the last couple of weeks. And he believed he'd seen a change in her. Where she'd been reserved and even a bit prickly toward him at first, once he'd gotten to know the woman beneath the impeccable designer suits, he'd found complicated layers of ambition, passion and vulnerability that intrigued him but also made him leery of moving too fast.

Her walls went up and came down in ever-fluctuating responses to ways he behaved and how deeply he plumbed her emotions. Yet now as he wondered about London's views on the future of their relationship, Harrison accepted he couldn't walk away from what they'd begun. He wasn't a quitter. And she was a woman worth fighting for.

"There you are." London's overly bright smile couldn't hide the shadows darkening her gold-flecked blue eyes. "I've been looking all over for you."

"I'm glad you found me."

Harrison put out his hand and smiled as London slipped hers into it. Ten days earlier she would've resisted doing something this simple and profoundly intimate. Her level of comfort with him had come a long way in a short period of time. Yet he couldn't shake the feeling that things were ever on the verge of swinging back.

"Did you have fun?" he asked.

"I did. Makes me want to take up polo."

"Really?" He'd like to see her barreling down the field, mallet swinging. "Do you ride?"

"I used to when I was younger. My dad taught me. He loves to hunt." A girlish smile curved her lips. "You know, ride to the hounds."

"They still do that?"

"Tuesdays, Thursdays and Sundays during season."

Harrison shook his head in bemusement. "Who knew?"

"Can we get out of here?" she asked, catching him by surprise. "I want to be alone with you."

"Nothing would make me happier."

But a nagging thought in the back of his mind left him questioning whether she was eager to be with him or just looking to escape an event where her ex was with someone else.

It didn't help that she seemed unusually preoccupied during the return trip to Charleston.

"Anything in particular you want to do?" he asked, breaking the silence as the car rolled along King Street. "It's not too early to grab a drink."

"Sure. Where do you want to go?"

"The Gin Joint or Proof?"

"The Gin Joint, I think."

Fifteen minutes later they'd settled into one of the booths in the cozy bar and ordered two quintessential Gin Joint drinks. The bar prided itself on its craft cocktails, seasonally updated, with clever names like Gutter Sparrow, Whiplash, Whirly Bird and Lucky Luciano.

"Delicious," London commented after taking a sip of her Continental Army cocktail, featuring apple brandy, caraway orgeat, lime, Seville orange, falernum, sugar and muddled apple. "The perfect fall drink."

Silence fell between them as they sipped their cocktails and contemplated the snack menu. Harrison debated whether to bring up the topic of her ex and the issues bothering him.

"I'm just going to come out and ask," he said abruptly, causing London to look up from the menu in surprise. "Today after you saw Linc, you seemed distracted and upset."

Her eyes widened. "I wasn't."

She was a terrible liar, but he decided against pressing her. Instead, he turned to another burning question.

"Have you spoken with your mother about us?" Harrison winced at his blunt delivery. "I'm asking because

I see a future for us." And he wanted to know what stood in the way.

"You do?" If it was possible, she looked even more stunned.

"I think about you all the time when we're not together and that's never happened to me before."

"But we barely know each other."

Concern lashed at him. Were they on the same page or not?

"I'm not saying I want to get married tomorrow, but I can't see an end to this thing between us and that's saying a lot." He leaned forward and fixed his eyes on her. "I need to know if you feel the same way."

"I…don't…know. That is…" She redirected her focus to the tabletop and an agonized expression passed over her features. "I do like you. A lot. But I haven't given any thought to the future."

Harrison sat back, unsatisfied by her answer. While he had to give her props for being honest, it wasn't the ringing endorsement of their connection he'd been hoping for.

"Then you'd be the first woman I've dated who hadn't," he said, fighting annoyance that he'd opened up while she remained guarded. "Is it because of what I do?"

"You mean racing? No." When he snorted in disbelief, she reached both her hands across the table and laid them over his. "My engagement ended a couple months ago after I'd been with Linc for three years. I was just starting to figure out who I am when you came into my life."

"I think that's crap. You know exactly who you are. The question is whether or not that woman can see herself with a guy like me. I'm not someone your mother would approve of. I don't have any interest in making the rounds of Charleston society. Our daughter would never attend a single debutante event. But I can promise I wouldn't ever make you regret a single day of our life together."

"Harrison…" She blinked rapidly and heaved a sigh.

"You have to decide what's truly important to you."

"You make me sounds like such a snob," she murmured, her high color betraying her inner turmoil. "I know what people say about me. That I wasn't in love with Linc. And that's probably true. There's a good reason why we were engaged for two years without ever setting a wedding date. But then there's the part where I think he was cheating on me." London's voice shook as she finished, "What if I don't have what it takes to keep a man interested long-term?"

Her words flattened Harrison against the booth seat. Was that what was bothering her? That she believed herself undesirable? How was that possible when he'd shown her over and over how much he wanted her?

"You have what it takes to keep the right man interested long-term. You chose the wrong guy last time. Have faith in what you want and who you are." He turned his hands over so that their palms rested against each other. It wrenched his heart that she couldn't bring herself to meet his gaze. "You have what it takes to keep me interested forever."

Her breath caught. "You shouldn't say things like that."

"Why not? You don't think I'm being truthful?"

"I think you have a lot to learn about me and what you discover might change your mind."

He couldn't imagine what she was talking about and had no idea how to coax her out of this sudden funk she'd fallen into. "I guess that could be said of me, as well. All I'm asking is for you to be open to exploring who we could be to each other."

"I can do that." She gave his hands a brief hard squeeze and let go. After a large swallow of her cocktail, she fastened a bright smile on her face and said, "How about you and I go back to my place and do some of that exploring you were talking about."

Grinning, Harrison threw a hundred on the table and got to his feet, holding out his hand. "Let's go."

Harrison didn't know what to expect when they got to her condo. London had sent him smoking-hot glances the entire drive. Now the door was barely shut before she backed him toward the foyer wall and then gave a shove that sent the breath whooshing from his lungs. A second later she pressed her body against his, gripping his hair in a painful grasp while crushing her lips to his. She kissed him hard and rough, making his world go black and hot. Blood rushed through his veins, pounding in his ears as she ambushed his senses with teeth and tongue and ragged breath.

He was helpless to process the astonishing hunger that gripped her. All he could do was surrender to her feasting and let her set him on fire.

Sinking his fingers into her silky hair, he savored the soft texture while his other hand slid down her back and slipped over the curve of her butt, lifting her against his growing erection. The move caused her to shudder and suck his lower lip between her teeth. A searing nip, followed by the soothing flick of her tongue, made him groan.

"I'm going to make you come like you never have," she whispered in his ear while her fingers raked down his torso until they encountered his belt.

He was a fan of dirty talk, and her words slammed into him, sending blood rushing to his groin. He'd never expected to hear London speak so boldly or to want to be in charge. It turned him on.

"I look forward to it," he said, throwing her over his shoulder and heading to the bedroom so they could get the party started.

She squawked at the undignified carry, and from the expression on her face as he set her on her feet beside the bed, she intended to make him pay. Harrison stripped off his jacket and tie, and then went to work on his shirt buttons. He couldn't wait for her to do her worst.

By the time he'd kicked off his shoes, her clothes were in a neat pile on the dresser and she was naked. Hands on hips, she watched him drop his pants to the floor and step out of them. When her gaze dropped to the erection straining his boxer briefs, a little smile formed on her lips.

Harrison frowned as he tried to make out the significance of her expression. If he'd believed he had London all figured out, he'd been wrong. This was a new side of her. The woman who took charge when it came to her work was obviously capable of stepping up in the bedroom, as well. He found himself impatient to see what came next.

She stalked toward him and grabbed a handful of his boxers, tugging the cotton material over his jutting erection and down his thighs. He hissed as the cool air caressed his heated flesh, but the chill was short-lived as her fingers closed around him. The tight grip and firm stroke that followed felt out-of-this-world fantastic.

"On the bed, so I can get these the rest of the way off you."

"Yes, ma'am."

He did as she asked, admiring the way her breasts swayed as she stripped him bare. Like some sort of wild thing, she peered at him from between the glossy strands of hair that hung across her face as she tossed his briefs aside. Straightening, she put her hands on her hips, surveying him with a wicked half smile.

"Ready?" she asked, not waiting for his nod before bending over the bed.

"Drive me crazy with your delightful tongue," he growled, his voice a guttural rasp.

One corner of her lips kicked up in a smirk. She scraped her fingernails up his thighs and his mouth went dry. She obviously wanted to steer the ship and he was dying to see what happened next. Fortunately, he didn't have long to wait.

Lust blasted through him as her lips dropped toward the head of his erection, but instead of taking him into her mouth, she hovered millimeters above. The anticipation was almost too painful and it struck home that she intended to take her time with him.

A low curse passed his lips as she flicked her tongue out and swirled it over him. Harrison's hips came off the mattress as she followed that with a long stroke down his shaft and then back up. Placing her hands on his knees, she pushed them wider before crawling forward to set up between his thighs.

For a second his breath lodged in his throat as she gently cupped his balls and then her mouth swooped down again, sucking him into a hot, wet tunnel that made him groan and shudder. She swirled her tongue around his erection and pleasure detonated through him.

Speaking…was impossible.

Thinking… Incoherent chants filled his mind.

He was tumbling, falling into an upside-down world where his desire and pleasure were less important than the sheer bliss of catching her gaze and realizing she was enjoying watching his reaction.

Although he longed to close his eyes so he could better focus on the sensations pounding through him, the picture of her hair splayed over his stomach and thighs, her lips locked around him, was a sight to behold.

Her blue eyes sparkled as she glanced up at him. She was filled with naughty surprises. Tremors rolled through his body as he realized she was enjoying this as much as he was. He curved his fingers around her head as his stomach muscles tightened. Skin on fire, he fought to hold on, to make the moment last. But the flames licked him, spreading through his veins, consuming him. Her tongue swirled around his erection and the first shock wave washed over him. Then another. Her mouth felt so damned good.

"Coming." A curse ripped through his mind. "Coming hard."

And then a climax barreled through his body, crashing wildly into bone and muscle and nerves. The unleashed power of it obliterated words and stopped his heart. For several seconds he rocketed through supercharged joy while aftershocks jolted him.

He wasn't even aware that she'd released him until her lips trailed over his chest and slid into the hollow of his throat where his pulse slammed against his skin.

"Amazing." His voice cracked on the one word.

Enough strength had returned to his muscles to allow him to gather her naked body against his. He drifted kisses along her hairline as he slowly recovered.

"Damn, woman," he murmured, cupping her cheek in his palm and bringing their lips together. He kept the kiss light and romantic, showing his appreciation. "You're good as your word. I think I blacked out for a second."

"You're easy," she told him. "You seem to enjoy everything."

He lifted his head off the pillow and regarded her in bemusement. "If by 'everything' you mean your gorgeous mouth on me, then you have that right. You make me come like I never have before," he told her, echoing her earlier promise. "It's different with you."

She looked shell-shocked, and even as he watched, she began withdrawing behind her emotional walls. "You don't need to say that…"

"Do I strike you as someone who says things he doesn't mean?"

"No."

"Then believe me when I tell you I'm in over my head here. I don't know what you do to me, but I like it."

"You do things to me, too," she replied, her long lashes concealing her eyes. "And I like it."

As she spoke, she stretched her lean body, making him keenly aware of her silky skin, renewing his desire. Harrison rolled her beneath him and tangled their legs, his lips finding that spot on her neck that made her shiver.

"Good to hear," he murmured, "because I'm going to spend the rest of the night doing all sorts of things to you. And I think we'll both like that."

It was nearly two in the morning and Everly sat in her car outside a twenty-four-hour drugstore, tearing apart the packaging to get to the prepaid cell phone she'd just purchased. It was important that the call she was about to make couldn't be tracked back to her.

She'd been thinking about this step for two days, weighing the options and debating if such a radical move would be beneficial to their plans. In the end, she'd decided that London needed to be punished. Her failure to use the flash drive to pull the information off Tristan's computer proved that not only her priorities had shifted but also her loyalty.

How was Zoe supposed to get her revenge if London didn't do her part? More important, what was the motivation for Zoe to take down Ryan if nothing bad happened to Tristan? And Everly really needed Zoe to enact some truly devastating vengeance on Ryan for what he'd done to Kelly.

Everly had kept to her part of the bargain. Satisfaction lay curled like a sleeping house cat in her chest. She was nearly purring with pleasure at the damage she'd caused.

In the midst of the charity polo event, she'd ruined Linc Thurston's life by showing him the truth about his housekeeper, ending their ridiculous romance.

No doubt by now, with Claire's past catching up to her in a big way, exposing all her lies and deceptions, Linc was feeling devastated and more than a little stupid that he'd been taken in so easily by an obvious opportunist.

In some way, Everly had actually done him a favor. Not that he'd thank her if he knew she'd been the one who'd contacted Claire's family and let them know where she was.

The look on Linc's face when he'd realized that Claire had lied to him about everything had given Everly such a thrill. She'd planned and executed a flawless plan and the results had been better than she could have imagined.

But not everyone had the strength of will to follow through. That had become crystal clear with the way London had chosen her romance with Harrison over loyalty to the plan. And now she would pay.

Everly keyed the play button on her phone and London's voice rang out with clear conviction.

I've used Harrison to get to Tristan. He means nothing to me except as a means to an end.

Everly dialed a number on the burner phone and waited for the call to roll to voice mail. She'd chosen the late hour, knowing Harrison would be occupied with London. The two of them had been spending all their time together, and after watching them at the polo event, it was pretty clear Harrison was falling for the event planner. And she for him.

Well, falling in love hadn't been part of the plan. London should've kept her clothes on and her focus on what they were trying to achieve.

"You've reached Harrison. I'm not available right now, but leave me your name and a brief message and I'll get back to you."

Smiling, Everly hit Play.

Ten

London woke to a soft morning light stealing past the gauzy curtains of her bedroom. She loved that her windows faced east. Waking up to the sunrise always boosted her optimism. The soothing palette of peach, pink, lavender and soft gold offered a tranquil beginning to her day. She often took a cup of coffee onto her broad terrace and sucked in a heady lungful of river breezes.

Stretching out her hand to the far side of the bed, she found the space empty and the sheets cool. Sighing, she pushed to a sitting position and ran her fingers through her tangled hair. Usually she braided it at night, but Harrison said he loved the spill of her satiny locks over his skin and she adored the way he tunneled his fingers through it.

She slipped from bed and donned a silky robe before following her nose to the kitchen, where the smell of coffee promised a large mug of dark roast. But as she neared the kitchen, the sound of her own voice reached her ears.

I've used Harrison to get to Tristan. He means nothing to me except as a means to an end.

She stopped dead, a malignant lump of dread forming in her chest as she remembered when she'd made that declaration. What did Everly think she was doing?

In her kitchen, Harrison stood at the island, one hand braced on the marble countertop while he stared at the phone. He looked like he'd been told he could never race again.

It was the same devastated look Linc had worn at the polo event during the brutal incident with Claire.

A rushing noise filled her ears as the edges of her vision grew fuzzy. She must've made a sound because his gaze whipped in her direction.

"What is this about?" he demanded, holding up his phone. "Why did you say those things?"

Even if she could speak, she had no words to explain.

"Damn it, London." His voice broke on her name. "I thought we had something."

She had to reply. He deserved an explanation. But would he listen? London doubted she'd be open to it if their situation were reversed.

"It isn't like it sounds—"

"Don't lie to me. I want to know what's really going on."

Gathering a huge breath, she stepped up to the kitchen

island and set her hands on it, leaning forward. "I'm trying to find out if your brother is hiding money."

"Why?"

She bit her lip. They'd promised not to tell anyone about what they were doing. Yet hadn't Everly broken their pact when she'd sent that audio clip to Harrison? What more could the woman do? Taint London's reputation? Bad-mouth ExcelEvent?

In the end, cowardice ruled. "I'm not at liberty to tell you."

For long, agonizing seconds he stared at her in silence, confusion and annoyance chasing across his features. "Why?"

"Because it's not my story to tell."

"So, us…?" The unformed question drained all animation from his eyes. "Was I a means to an end?"

She could try lying to him, but he knew her well enough by now to see right through it. "At first."

He took the hit without reacting. "I suppose you want me to believe that things changed."

"They did. I would never have…" She hesitated, unsure what came next. Thanks to the revenge bargain she'd become unrecognizable to herself.

"Never would have…?" He prompted. "Slept with me? Led me to believe your feelings for me were real?" Although his tone remained neutral, the tension around his eyes and the muscle jumping in his jaw displayed what was really going on inside him.

"I do have feelings for you."

But even as the claim left her lips, London saw it

was too little and too late. Harrison's eyes hardened to flint, and her heart stopped.

"You don't understand," she protested.

He appeared impervious to her desperate plea. "Then tell me what's going on."

"I can't." Trapped between her mistakes and her longing to come clean, London closed her eyes and wished herself back in time to that fateful women's empowerment function. How had she believed that doing something wrong would make anything better?

"You mean you won't," Harrison countered.

"It's complicated."

The lame excuse bought her no sympathy. Harrison crossed his arms over his chest and regarded her in disgust.

"Can you at least explain to me why you're doing this?"

Maybe it would help if she did. She couldn't tell him everything, but she could say enough that maybe he'd understand.

"I'm helping a friend. Your brother hurt her and I'm trying to…" This is where her story got murky. London no longer believed that what she, Zoe and Everly were doing would make any of them any better off.

"Hurt him back?" Harrison guessed.

London found it hard to meet his gaze. "That's the way it started."

"And things are different now?"

"Yes and no. There's no question that Tristan is a bad guy who did bad things. I'm just not sure doing bad things to a bad guy is the answer. How is it helping anyone to get back at him?"

"I'll be the first one to admit that my brother has not always been a decent individual and I turned a blind eye to a lot of his behavior."

For a second London thought that maybe Harrison understood and could forgive her, but there was no sympathy in his eyes. Only regret.

"Your comments about his spending habits at the polo match got me thinking. I'm not sure if he's been engaged in questionable activities, and I sure as hell hope it has nothing to do with Crosby Automotive, but he's spending above and beyond his income." Harrison rubbed his hand over his eyes. "And I know he treated Zoe badly. She didn't deserve his abuse while they were married or to be discarded the way she was."

"She didn't have an affair. It was something Tristan trumped up to get out of paying her a fair settlement."

"I never believed she did and I should've spoken up on her behalf. She deserved better than she got."

London remained quiet as Harrison's eyes narrowed. His statements struck close to the heart of her motivation.

"Was Zoe the one you were helping?" Harrison asked after a long span of silence.

Her instincts urged her to trust him even as she doubted her purpose in doing so. Did she hope he'd forgive her if he knew what they'd been up to? And how would he feel about what Everly had done to Linc on London's behalf? And what if Everly got wind of the fact that she'd confided in Harrison? What insane stunt would she pull then?

"Talk to me," he said, softening his tone. "What the hell is going on?"

London chewed on her lip, fear of the consequences paralyzing her. At long last she sighed.

"All I can say is that I was trying to find out the truth about your brother's financial situation. It seems likely that he's hiding money because it's pretty common knowledge that Zoe didn't get anywhere near the settlement she should have."

"And how did you think you could do that?" Harrison asked.

"He has to keep track of things somehow. I thought by gaining access to his computer I could find everything I needed."

Harrison frowned. "That's absurd. Didn't you realize he'd have his computer and his files password protected?"

"I have something that's supposed to get past that."

"What?"

She went to her purse, pulled out the USB drive and held it up. "This. It's some kind of special program that was supposed to get me past his security."

Harrison came toward her, gaze fixed on the drive. "Where did you get it?"

With her eyes begging him to understand, London shook her head.

A muscle jumped in Harrison's jaw. "How does it work?"

She explained the process and he held out his hand. "Give me the drive."

Meek as a lamb, London handed it over. "I'm sorry,"

she whispered. "Please don't tell Tristan. If he finds out, he'll make things worse for Zoe."

If her plea had any effect on him, nothing showed in his expression. He remained furious, but London hoped a shred of affection for her had survived and he wouldn't do anything to cause her harm.

Harrison turned the flash drive over and over in his hand, contemplating it. "My brother doesn't need to know about this. But I'm keeping this and you will stay away from him."

Relief flooded her. Nothing suited London more than backing away from the whole situation. Then she remembered that her problems weren't limited to Tristan. Everly had sent Harrison the snippet of their conversation as a warning shot. London still had to contend with her.

"What are you going to do with the drive?" she asked.

"I don't know." He dropped it into his pocket. "The only thing I'm sure of at the moment is that you and I are done."

Harrison drove the familiar roads to Crosby Motorsports, seeking comfort in what he knew and loved. Cars and racing had always been his go-to when things got hard. He'd lost track of how many hours he'd spent as a kid with a wrench in his hand, learning how to tear apart something and then putting it back together. There was security in the logic of how the pieces fit together, each with a particular purpose. As he'd reached an age when he spent more time behind the wheel than under the hood, his appreciation had grown for a perfectly functioning car.

Unfortunately, in the racing world, as much as they strove to have everything work smoothly, that rarely happened. Bolts loosened. Suspensions failed. Brakes gave out. Drivers trained for when things went wrong, when systems failed or other drivers made mistakes. Situations didn't always have to spin out of control.

The other side of the coin from preparation was luck. Harrison considered himself fortunate that during his career while he'd been involved in several wrecks, he'd walked away from all but one of them. Yet despite the danger inherent in his sport, he never questioned getting behind the wheel of number twenty-five.

Too bad life wasn't equally easy to prepare for and navigate. Nothing he'd ever experienced could've enabled Harrison to see the wreck between him and London coming. She'd completely blindsided him. One second he was in his lane, thinking that he had everything in hand, and the next he was spinning out of control on a trajectory that sent him crashing into the wall.

Ahead of him the entrance gate to Crosby Motorsports came into view. As he sped onto the property, the peace he'd always gathered from being there eluded him. The facility had been more than his home away from home for nearly two decades. It was the center of his world. Yet tonight as he pulled up in front of the engine shop, his heart wasn't here.

He expected the building to be empty. With the season done, the team had headed home for some much-needed rest and family time. Harrison used his keycard to access the engine shop and easily navigated the familiar space in the dim light. Of all the various components that went into the cars, he had a particular fondness for engines since his earliest memories were of working beside his uncle, learning how all the complicated parts came together to move the vehicle forward in breathtaking speeds.

Of course, the engines designed and built by the Crosby Motorsports team were far more sophisticated than the engines Harrison had learned on. These days the engines were customized each week for the particular racetrack based on the speed and throttle characteristics and even the driver.

"What are you doing here?"

Looking past the neat row of engines lined up along one wall, Harrison spied his uncle headed his way.

"Just clearing my head."

"How's London? Things going okay?"

"Why do you ask?"

"She's the first woman you've brought around in a long time. I figured she was someone special." Jack removed his ball cap and ran slender fingers through his thick gray hair. "And with the hangdog look about you right now, it stands to reason that something went wrong."

With the season over, Jack became a lot more approachable, and Harrison decided to take advantage of his uncle's years of experience being married to a firecracker like Dixie.

"When London and I first started dating, I thought our biggest problem was going to be that she wouldn't give me a chance because I didn't have the sort of Charleston social connections she was looking to make."

"And now?" Jack asked, not looking a bit surprised.

"I think those issues are still there, but they aren't the biggest problem we have."

Jack shook his head in disgust and suddenly Harrison was an impulsive teenager again, eager to get behind the wheel of a car he couldn't handle.

"Do you think for one second if I hadn't fought for Dixie that we'd be together right now?" Jack asked. "Your dad and I had empty pockets and big dreams when I met your aunt."

"But she married you," Harrison reminded him.

"You say that like there was never any question she would. Her dad chased me off their property the first time I made her cry."

Harrison regarded his uncle in shock, intrigued by this glimpse into Jack's personal life. Usually his uncle stuck to tales about the business or racing and Harrison sensed there was a good story waiting to be told.

"You made her cry?" He couldn't imagine his tough-as-nails aunt reduced to tears. "Why? How?"

"I wasn't the smooth operator I am today."

Harrison snorted. His uncle often told stories, and the more dramatic the circumstances, the better. Not everything was 100 percent true, but there was enough reality to provide a moral. The key was discovering what exactly to believe.

"So, what happened?"

"She was debuting and wanted me as her escort for

the ball. We'd been going out for only a few months at the time and I certainly wasn't her parents' first choice."

"Did you do something to embarrass her at the event?"

"I never made it to the ball."

"Why?"

"Stupid pride." Jack's expression turned sheepish. "I turned her down. She and I were from different worlds. I believed if we went together, she'd be the target of ridicule and I didn't want to put her through that."

Harrison winced. That same thought had crossed his mind at Richmond Raceway when he'd glimpsed London there. It had been so obvious that she didn't fit in. And later when he'd seen her with his brother at the Crosby Motorsports party, he'd briefly wondered if she'd prefer to be with someone who shared similar business and social connections.

"If that's what you believed," Harrison asked, "why did you start dating her in the first place?"

"Because she turned my world upside down. I could no more stay away from her than stop breathing. She was my heart and my reason for getting up every morning."

Jack's words hit closer to home than Harrison would've liked.

"So what happened after you turned down her invitation to attend the ball?"

"I'd underestimated how strong she was. And how determined. She didn't give a damn what other people thought. She was proud of me, of the man I was, and wanted everyone to know it." Jack raked his fingers through his hair as regret twisted his features. Even now, after more than three decades of wedded bliss, Harrison could see his uncle wished he'd behaved a different way. "My actions made it appear that I believed her choices were flawed. And that I didn't trust her."

"But she married you, so she must have gotten over it," Harrison said.

"It took a year."

Harrison could imagine what those months must've been like for his uncle. He was experiencing his own separation angst at the moment.

"You must have been really hung up on her to have stayed in the fight that long," he said.

"You know, at the beginning of the year I don't believe I understood what I was feeling. Plus, if I'd been truly in love or, more to the point, been willing to surrender my stubbornness and give in to my emotions, I might have saved myself a lot of pain."

Harrison didn't want to ponder an entire year away from London, so he asked, "Why did you keep going when she rejected you for a year?"

"Because to be without her hurt more than my foolish pride. I tried to stay away, but rarely lasted more than a week or two. Life got pretty bleak for me, pretty fast. It also made me more determined to be worthy of her. That's when Crosby Automotive really started to take off. I threw every bit of my frustration and fear and joy into making something I could be proud of. I thought if I was wealthy and successful that I could win her back."

"Did it work?"

Jack shook his head. "It made things worse. The better Crosby Automotive did, the more confident I became and the less she wanted to have anything to do with me."

Harrison wasn't liking where the story was going. "So what did it take?"

"She started dating someone perfect for her. A guy from a wealthy, well-connected family." Jack's expression hardened. "I fell into a dark well for a couple of weeks."

"How'd you come out of it?"

"I weighed being happy for the rest of my life against my pride."

"And?" Harrison didn't really need to ask. He saw where his uncle was going. "What did it take?"

"The most difficult conversation of my life. I had to completely open myself up to her. Fears, hopes, how she made my life better and that I wanted to be worthy of her love."

Strong emotion filled Jack's voice even after three and a half decades. The power of it drove Harrison's misery higher. His throat tightened, preventing him from speaking for a long moment.

Into the silence, his uncle spoke again. "Is what you feel for her worth fighting for?"

Could he live without London? Probably. Would it be any fun? Doubtful. For so long racing had been his purpose and passion. He'd never considered that he'd sacrificed anything to be at the top of his game. But was that true?

With London he'd started thinking in terms of family and kids, and there was no question that she'd pulled his focus away from racing. The telling part was that he didn't mind. In fact, he'd begun to think in terms of how he intended to make changes in his schedule next year to spend as much time with her as possible. He suspected that if this business with his brother hadn't gotten between them, he'd be well on his way to looking at engagement rings.

"For a long time I thought so." Harrison's chest tightened at the thought of letting her go, but he couldn't imagine how to get past the way she'd used him. He'd never been one to hold a grudge, but trusting her again seemed hopeless. "Now I'm not so sure."

Eleven

A subdued and thoroughly disgraced London entered the Cocktail Club on King Street and searched the animated crowd for her best friend. Maribelle had grabbed two seats at the bar. As London made her way through the customers, Maribelle was flashing her engagement ring at a persistent admirer.

These days because of the magic of Maribelle's true love glow, members of both sexes flocked to her. By comparison, London felt dull and sluggish. She couldn't sleep, wasn't eating and couldn't remember the last time she'd exercised.

"Holy hell," Maribelle exclaimed as London slid onto the bar stool beside her. "You look awful." She narrowed her eyes and looked her friend up and down. "Are you ready to tell me what happened?"

It had been ten days since that horrible morning when Harrison had received that damning audio clip from Everly.

As London filled her in, Maribelle's expression underwent several transformations from shock to dismay and finally irritation, but she didn't interrupt until London's story wound to its bitter finish.

"He's never going to speak to me again," London said, putting the final nail in the coffin that held the most amazing romance of her life.

"And well he shouldn't." Maribelle scowled. "I'm a little tempted never to speak to you again, either."

Knowing her friend didn't really mean that, London sat in rebuked silence while Maribelle signaled the bartender and ordered two shots of tequila.

"You know I can't drink that," London protested as the shots were delivered along with salt and limes. "Remember what happened the last time."

"I do and you are going to drink it until you're drunk enough to call Harrison and tell him the whole story, after which you're going to beg for his forgiveness. And then I'm going to take you home and hold your hair while you throw up." Maribelle handed her the shot. "Because that's what best friends do."

"I love you," London murmured, nearly blind from the grateful tears gathering in her eyes.

"I know. Now drink."

It took two shots in close succession and twenty minutes for London's dread to unravel. Two more and an hour before London found enough confidence to do the right thing.

"I'm going to regret this in the morning," London muttered, picking her phone up off the bar. The roiling in her stomach had nothing to do with the tequila she'd consumed. Yet.

"I know." Maribelle's voice was sympathetic, but she maintained the steely demeanor of a drill sergeant. "Now call."

Beneath Maribelle's watchful eye, London unlocked her phone and pulled up Harrison's contact information. With her heart trying to hammer its way out of her chest, she tapped on his name. As his handsome face lit up her screen, she almost chickened out. Maribelle must have sensed this because she made the same chastising sound she used to correct the new puppy she and Beau had just adopted.

London put the phone to her ear and reminded herself to breathe. Facing Harrison after what she'd done to him ranked as the hardest thing she'd ever had to do. But she owed him the full truth and so much more.

"I didn't think I'd hear from you again."

She almost burst into ugly sobs as his deep voice filled her ear and suddenly her throat was too tight for her to speak.

"Hello? London, are you there?" He paused. "Or have you butt-dialed me while you're out having a good time? It sounds like you're at a party."

Someone behind her had a rowdy laugh that blasted through the bar right on cue.

"I'm not having fun." Not one bit. *I miss you.* "I have things to tell you. Can I come over so I can explain some things to you?"

He remained silent for so long, she expected him to turn her down.

"I'm home now."

"I can't tonight," she said, glancing at the line of empty shot glasses. "Tonight, I'm going to be very, very sick."

Again he paused before answering. "Tomorrow afternoon, then?"

"At two?"

"At two."

The line went dead and London clapped her hand over her mouth before making a beeline for the bathroom.

At a little after two the following afternoon, Harrison opened the door to his penthouse unit and immediately cursed the way his heart clenched at the sight of London. From her red-rimmed eyes to her pale skin and lopsided topknot, she looked as miserable as he felt.

To his dismay, instead of venting his irritation, his first impulse was to haul her into the foyer and wrap her in his arms. Her gaze clung to him as he stepped back and gestured her inside.

Due to the turn in the weather, she'd dressed in jeans, soft suede boots and a bulky sweater in sage green. From her pink cheeks and windblown hair, he suspected she'd walked over from her building along the waterside thoroughfare that ran beside the Cooper River.

With the front door closed, the spacious foyer seemed to narrow. Beneath the scent of wind and water that she'd brought into his home, her perfume tickled his nostrils. Abruptly, he was overwhelmed by memories. Of the joyful hours she'd spent here. The long nights they'd devoured each other. The lazy Sunday mornings when they'd talked over coffee, croissants and egg-white omelets.

"Thank you for letting me come over," she murmured.

Harrison shoved his hands into his pockets. He would not touch her or offer comfort of any kind, no matter how soft and sweet and vulnerable she looked. He would not let her off easy or tell her it was okay, because it wasn't.

"You said you wanted to explain about going after my brother," he growled. "So explain."

"I will, but first I need to say something to you." London's beautiful eyes clung to him. "When I'm with you, I feel…everything. I didn't expect all the things you make me want and need. I didn't understand that once we'd made love there would be no going back for me."

Harrison's muscles quivered and it took willpower to prevent his body from responding to what she was saying. Her every word echoed how he'd felt about her and the loss he'd experienced these last few days gripped him anew.

"All I want is to be with you." Her hands fluttered, graceful as a dancer's, opening and closing as she poured out her emotions. "You made me feel beautiful and fulfilled. You gave me a safe place to be open and vulnerable."

"That's not an explanation for why you used me,"

he said, his heart wrenching so hard it was difficult to keep a grip on his impatience.

Her expression was a study in consternation as she began again. "I was afraid to tell you what I was doing for fear that you'd hate me."

Her declaration shook him to the core.

"I could never hate you."

He loved her.

The realization left him stunned and reeling. For days he'd ignored the part of him that had recognized the signs

"Harrison, I'm sorry," London said, her voice sounding very far away even though she stood within reach. "I did a terrible thing."

He loved her?

How was that possible given what she'd done?

She'd used him to get to his brother. Didn't she know he would've done anything for her if only she'd asked? His soul ached as he resisted his heart's longing for her. She would always be his weakness.

Needing to put some distance between them before he succumbed to the urge to back her against the wall and lose himself in her, Harrison marched back toward his living room.

It wasn't until he threw himself onto the couch that he realized she hadn't left the foyer. With an impatient huff, he rose and went to find her. She stood where he'd left her, pulling down her sleeves to hide her hands.

"I'm so deeply sorry that what I did hurt you," she said, her voice tiny and choked with tears. "And I want to tell you everything."

"You might as well come in and tell me the whole story."

Losing the battle to avoid touching her, Harrison towed London into the living room and drew her to the couch. Once they were seated side by side, she began her tale.

"It all started when I met Zoe and another woman, Everly Briggs, at a networking event a few months ago. We were all strangers and each of us was in a bad place. Linc had just broken off our engagement. Zoe's divorce was going badly. And Everly claimed her sister had been wrongly imprisoned."

London's fingers clenched and flexed in her lap. "I don't know who first brought up the idea of getting back at the men who'd hurt us, but Everly jumped pretty hard on it and her enthusiasm swept up both Zoe and me."

Harrison hated that London's pain from her broken engagement had driven her to do something reckless.

"Zoe was pretty scared of Tristan and I didn't want to go after Linc and damage my reputation by appearing vindictive. So..." She blew out a big breath. "Since we were strangers who met by chance, we decided to take on each other's men. Everly went after Linc for me. I went after Tristan for Zoe. And she's supposed to take down Ryan Dailey for Everly."

Despite his dismay at her story, Harrison could see the logic in their approach. "So who sent me the audio clip of you?"

"Everly. She wanted to make you hate me." London peered at him anxiously. "She saw how important you were becoming to me."

His treacherous heart sang as some of his hurt and anger eased at her confession. The longing to take her in his arms grew more urgent, but he resisted. Although it was clear that no matter what she'd done or why, he couldn't stop wanting her, he required a full explanation before deciding what to do next.

"So where do things stand now?"

"I don't know. Obviously, I wasn't up to fulfilling my part of the bargain and you can see how Everly reacted to that." London made a face. "I feel terrible for Zoe. Among the three of us, what happened to her was the most damaging."

"Didn't you say Everly's sister went to jail?"

"Yes, but from what I've been able to find out, she did something illegal. Maybe Ryan Dailey didn't have to go so far as to press charges, but his company lost several million dollars because of her and he was well within his rights."

London lapsed into silence, her gaze fixed on his chest, her downcast expression battering the walls he'd erected against her. Her genuine remorse left him grappling with her decision to take revenge on her ex-fiancé. What did that say about her?

Yet after suffering his own heartbreak, he was better able to sympathize with the pain she'd experienced. Dark emotions had taken him to irrational places unlike any he'd visited before she entered his life.

Harrison reached around to the sofa table behind him and picked up a manila envelope. The information it held put him square in the middle of London's trouble.

"Here," he said, handing her the envelope.

"What is this?" London's gaze flickered from his face to the envelope and back again.

"Open it up and see."

London unfastened the clasp and flipped up the flap to peer inside. "It looks like banking information."

"My brother's banking information," Harrison clarified. "Turns out Tristan had secret offshore accounts and shell corporations that he used to move money to the States. I don't know if the information will help Zoe, but it wasn't fair that Tristan hid these accounts from her."

While he spoke, she pulled several pages out and scanned them. "Why did you do this?"

"Zoe got a raw deal."

It wasn't his only motivation, but Harrison wasn't ready to say more. He'd done a lot of soul-searching before he'd betrayed his brother by using the flash drive and stealing these files. Although he remained conflicted about his decision, seeing the questionable legality of what Tristan had been up to had eased his conscience somewhat.

"This is a lot of money," London said. "I mean a lot of money. Way more than he should have been able to put away by regular means. Where do you suppose it came from?"

The question had been keeping Harrison up at night. He had yet to figure out what to do with the information he'd gathered, but knew a conversation with his father and uncle was in order.

"I think he's been laundering money," he said.

"Laundering money for whom?"

"Drug dealers. Russian mob." The more he'd re-
viewed the information, the more extreme his speculation had become and the more concerned he'd grown
about the potential repercussions for Crosby Automotive. "It's hard to say."

Her eyes went wide. "You don't seriously believe
your brother is doing something illegal, do you? How
could that be happening?"

"Crosby Automotive buys almost all its parts from
overseas manufacturers and my brother is responsible
for deciding which companies we buy from. It wouldn't
be impossible for him to channel bribes into one of these
offshore accounts."

"But does he need more money than he has?"

"You've seen his homes and his spending habits.
Tristan likes to live the life of a billionaire. 'Act like
you're worth a fortune and people will be inclined to believe it,'" he quoted in his brother's lofty tones. "Instead
it looks like he just went deeper and deeper into debt."

"Is Crosby Automotive in danger from what he's
been doing?"

"I don't think so." Harrison hoped not. It would be
something he'd need to address in coming months.

London shoved the pages back into the envelope.
"How can I thank you for this?"

"No need. What Tristan did to Zoe was wrong."

She set her hand on his. The move sent a zing of excitement through his body. He set his teeth against the
urge to pull her onto his lap and sink his fingers into
her tousled hair. His gaze slid to her full lips. One kiss
and he'd be beneath her spell once more. But...

"I'm so sorry for what I did," she said, forcing Harrison to rein in his lust-filled thoughts.

"Look, I've started to understand your motives."

"My motives in the beginning," she corrected him, turning his hand over so her fingers could trace evocative patterns on his palm. "Things changed when I got to know you."

Harrison's blood heated as she inched closer. The entreaty in her eyes undermined his willpower. "I get it, but I can't just go on as if none of this happened."

"I don't blame you." She peered at him from beneath her lashes. "But I just want you to know that you changed me in ways I never imagined possible."

"London…"

Before he knew it, Harrison found himself leaning in. Her feminine scent lured him closer still. He knew exactly where she applied her perfume. A dab on her neck, right over the madly throbbing pulse. Another behind her ear. The hollow of her elbow. Behind her knees.

"I know I have no right to ask, but could you ever…?" She bit her lip, unable to finish the question.

"Forgive you?" He was on the verge of forgetting everything except the driving need to delve into her heat as her palm coasted over his shoulder.

"I know it's not fair for me to ask. But if there's anything I can do." Her other hand found his thigh and Harrison almost groaned at the tornado of lust swirling in him. "If there's any way back to where we were," she continued. "Or forward to something better. All you need to do is tell me what you need me to do."

Harrison raked his fingers through his hair and blew

out a giant breath while his craving for her warred with his shattered faith.

"My uncle told me a story about when he and Dixie were dating. He did something wrong and spent the following year trying to get back in her good graces."

"If you think it'll take a year for you to forgive me," London said, so close now that it took no effort at all for her to slide her lips over his ear, "I'm for doing whatever it takes."

Harrison shuddered as her husky voice vibrated through him. "You'd make that pledge without knowing if I could ever trust you again?"

"I trust that the man you are will play fair with me." She tipped her head and let him see her conviction. "You are worth the risk."

With his ability to resist her unraveling, Harrison said, "You know, when we first started seeing each other I got the impression you didn't feel that way."

"That you were worth the risk?" She shook her head. "Maybe at the very beginning I judged you for what you did for a living. But you were willing to give me a chance anyway."

With a warm, willing woman sliding her hand farther up his thigh, Harrison couldn't figure out why he was still talking. But while his body was revving past safety limits, his heart hadn't yet recovered from crashing.

"You had great legs."

She shook her head at that. "I wasn't exactly your type, though, was I?"

"No. You were far too reserved."

They shared a grin at how much that had changed and more of Harrison's doubts began to fizzle and fade.

"If that was true, why did you approach me at the foundation event?" she asked, leaning more of her body against him.

"Truth?" He sighed as her soft breasts flattened against his arm. "Because you seemed interested in Tristan and I wanted to protect you from him."

"Seriously?" She eased back a fraction and shook her head in wonder. "So, if not for my ill-conceived plot against your brother, we never would've gone out."

"We might have." But he didn't really believe that.

"I don't think so," she said. "We were too different."

While she'd caught his eye at the event, he'd initially dismissed her as not his type. Odd that they'd both nearly let their prejudices get in the way of something amazing.

"That means," she continued, "in a fateful twist, the revenge plot brought us together."

Harrison considered that for a long moment. "I guess it did."

"I'm glad. I don't regret a single second of the time I spent falling in love with you."

"You what?" Her admission was unexpected.

She looked surprised that he didn't know this already. "I've fallen in love with you." Her voice gained confidence as she repeated herself. Drawing her feet under her, she got onto her knees and cupped his face. "I love you, Harrison Crosby. You are strong and thoughtful and sexy and just the best man I've ever known."

Abruptly, she stopped gushing compliments and

scanned his face, gauging his reaction. As their gazes locked, the last of Harrison's doubts washed away. This was the woman he was meant to be with. The proof was in the thunderous pounding of his heart and the exquisite openness of her expression.

This time, the impulse to put his arms around her was too strong. Harrison hauled her against him.

"I adore you," he murmured, burying his face in her hair. "You've shown me what's been missing in my life and I know now that I'll never be happy without you."

As their mouths fused, he felt as well as heard a half sob escape her, and then she was pushing into the kiss, her tongue finding its way into his mouth. He let her take the lead, enjoying the way his brain short-circuited as her hunger set him on fire.

His fingers dived beneath her sweater, finding bare skin. They groaned in unison as his thumbs brushed her tight nipples. He shifted their positions until she was flat on her back, her thighs parted and legs tangled with his. For a moment he ignored the compelling ache in his groin and smoothed silky strands of her hair away from her flushed face.

"I want to marry you," he said.

Her surprise lasted less than a heartbeat. "I'd like to marry you, too."

"You don't want to think about it?" He looked for some hint of doubt or hesitation in her manner, but only love and trust blazed in her eyes.

"I'm a better person when I'm with you," she said. "Why would I ever want to give that up?" She smiled then and it was the most beautiful thing he'd ever seen. "You're stuck with me."

"I'd say we're stuck with each other."

"And I don't want a long engagement."

"Lots of planes go to Las Vegas every day from the Charleston airport."

His suggestion briefly caught her off guard but then the most mischievous smile formed. "I'm feeling like the luckiest woman alive at the moment, so that sounds like a great idea."

He'd only been partially serious, but seeing that she was game, he nodded. In truth, he'd expected her to want to spend months planning an elaborate wedding to rival her friend's. "Just you and me?"

"Would you be upset if I invited Maribelle and Beau? I think she'd kill me if I got married without her."

"Let's give her a call."

"Later." London's lips moved to his neck even as she gave his butt a suggestive squeeze, pulling him hard against her. "Right now I want to make love with you."

Harrison nodded as his lips swept over hers, tasting her deliciously sweet mouth. As he wedged his erection against her, he could feel her smile and grinned in return as she rocked against him, inflaming both their desires.

Eventually he knew they would take things to the bedroom, but for now he was content to fool around on his couch like they were a couple of teenagers.

* * * * *

Cat Schield's
Sweet Tea & Scandal
series continues
with Zoe Crosby's story.

Don't miss it!

Available February 2019
from Harlequin Desire.

In her brand-new series, New York Times *bestselling author Brenda Jackson welcomes you to Catalina Cove, where even the biggest heartbreaks can be healed...*

Turn the page for a sneak peek at Love in Catalina Cove

CHAPTER ONE

New York City

VASHTI ALCINDOR SHOULD be celebrating. After all, the official letter she'd just read declared her divorce final, which meant her three-year marriage to Scott Zimmons was over. Definitely done with. As far as she was concerned the marriage had lasted two years too long. She wouldn't count that first year since she'd been too in love to dwell on Scott's imperfections. Truth be told there were many that she'd deliberately overlooked. She'd been so determined to have that happily-ever-after that she honestly believed she could put up with anything.

But reality soon crept into the world of make-believe, and she discovered she truly couldn't. Her husband was a compulsive liar who could look you right in the eyes and lie with a straight face. She didn't want to count the number of times she'd caught him in the act. When she couldn't take the deceptions any longer she had packed her things and left. When her aunt Shelby died five months later, Scott felt entitled to half of the inheritance Vashti received in the will.

It was then that Vashti had hired one of the best divorce attorneys in New York, and within six weeks his private investigator had uncovered Scott's scandalous activities. Namely, his past and present affair with his boss's wife. Vashti hadn't wasted any time making Scott aware that she was not only privy to this information, but had photographs and videos to prove it.

Knowing she wouldn't hesitate to expose him as the lowlife that he was, Scott had agreed to an uncontested divorce and walked away with nothing. The letter she'd just read was documented proof that he would do just about anything to hold on to his cushy Wall Street job.

Her cell phone ringing snagged her attention, the ringtone belonging to her childhood friend and present Realtor, Bryce Witherspoon. Vashti clicked on her phone as she sat down at her kitchen table with her evening cup of tea. "Hey, girl, I hope you're calling with good news."

Bryce chuckled. "I am. Someone from the Barnes Group from California was here today and—"

"California?"

"Yes. They're a group of developers that's been trying to acquire land in the cove for years. They made you an unbelievably fantastic offer for Shelby by the Sea."

Vashti let out a loud shout of joy. She couldn't believe she'd been lucky enough to get rid of both her ex-husband and her aunt's property in the same day.

"Don't get excited yet. We might have problems," Bryce said.

Vashti frowned. "What kind of problems?"

"The developers want to tear down your aunt's bed-and-breakfast and—"

"Tear it down?" Vashti felt a soft kick in her stomach. Selling her aunt's bed-and-breakfast was one thing, having it demolished was another. "Why would they want to tear it down?"

"They aren't interested in the building, Vash. They want the eighty-five acres it sits on. Who wouldn't with the Gulf of Mexico in its backyard? I told you it would be a quick sale."

Vashti had known someone would find Shelby by the Sea a lucrative investment but she'd hoped somehow the inn would survive. With repairs it could be good as new. "What do they want to build there instead?"

"A luxury tennis resort."

Vashti nodded. "How much are they offering?" she asked, taking a sip of her tea.

"Ten million."

Vashti nearly choked. "Ten million dollars? That's nearly double what I was asking for."

"Yes, but the developers are eyeing the land next to it, as well. I think they're hoping that one day Reid Lacroix will cave and sell his property. When he does, the developers will pounce on the opportunity to get their hands on it and build that golf resort they've been trying to put there for years. Getting your land will put their foot in the door so to speak."

Vashti took another sip of her tea. "What other problems are there?"

"This one is big. Mayor Proctor got wind of their offer and figured you might sell. He's calling a meeting."

"A meeting?"

"Yes, of the Catalina Cove zoning board. Although they can't stop you from selling the inn, they plan to block the buyer from bringing a tennis resort in here. The city ordinance calls for the zoning board to approve all new construction. This won't be the first time developers wanted to come into the cove and build something the city planners reject. Remember years ago when that developer wanted to buy land on the east end to build that huge shopping mall? The zoning board stopped it. They're determined that nothing in Catalina Cove changes."

"Well, it should change." As far as Vashti was concerned it was time for Mayor Proctor to get voted out. He had been mayor for over thirty years. When Vashti had left Catalina Cove for college fourteen years ago, developers had been trying to buy up the land for a number of progressive projects. The people of Catalina Cove were the least open-minded group she knew.

Vashti loved living in New York City where things were constantly changing and people embraced those changes. At eighteen she had arrived in the city to attend New York University and remained after getting a job with a major hotel chain. She had worked her way up to her six-figure salary as a hotel executive. At thirty-two she considered it her dream job. That wasn't bad for someone who started out working the concierge desk.

"Unless the Barnes Group can build whatever they want without any restrictions, there won't be a deal for us."

Vashti didn't like the sound of that. Ten million was ten million no matter how you looked at it. "Although I wouldn't want them to tear down Shelby, I think my aunt would understand my decision to do what's best for me." And the way Vashti saw it, ten million dollars was definitely what would be best for her.

"Do you really think she would want you to tear down the inn? She loved that place."

Vashti knew more than anyone how much Shelby by the Sea had meant to her aunt. It had become her life. "Aunt Shelby knew there was no way I would ever move back to Catalina Cove after what happened. Mom and Dad even moved away. There's no connection for me to Catalina Cove."

"Hey, wait a minute, Vash. I'm still here."

Vashti smiled, remembering how her childhood friend had stuck with her through thick and thin. "Yes, you're still there, which makes me think you need your head examined for not moving away when you could have."

"I love Catalina Cove. It's my home and need I remind you that for eighteen years it was yours, too."

"Don't remind me."

"Look, I know why you feel that way, Vash, but are you going to let that one incident make you have ill feelings about the town forever?"

"It was more than an incident, Bryce, and you know it." For Vashti, having a baby out of wedlock at sixteen had been a lot more than an incident. For her it had been a life changer. She had discovered who her real friends were during that time. Even now she would occasionally wonder how different things might have been had her child lived instead of died at birth.

"Sorry, bad choice of words," Bryce said, with regret in her voice.

"No worries. That was sixteen years ago." No need to tell Bryce that on occasion she allowed her mind to wander to that period of her life and often grieved for the child she'd lost. She had wanted children and Scott had promised they would start a family one day. That had been another lie.

"Tell me what I need to do to beat the rezoning board on this, Bryce," Vashti said, her mind made up.

"Unfortunately, to have any substantial input, you need to meet with the board in person. I think it will be beneficial if the developers make an appearance, as well. According to their representative, they're willing to throw in a few perks that the cove might find advantageous."

"What kind of perks?"

"Free membership to the resort's clubhouse for the first year, as well as free tennis lessons for the kids for a limited time. It will also bring a new employer to town, which means new jobs. Maybe if they were to get support from the townsfolk, the board would be more willing to listen."

"What do you think are our chances?"

"To be honest, even with all that, it's a long shot. Reid Lacroix is on the board and he still detests change. He's still the wealthiest person in town, too, and has a lot of clout."

"Then why waste my and the potential buyer's time?"

"There's a slim chance time won't be wasted. K-Gee is on the zoning board and he always liked you in school. He's one of the few progressive members on the board and the youngest. Maybe he'll help sway the others."

Vashti smiled. Yes, K-Gee had liked her but he'd liked Bryce even more and they both knew it. His real name was Kaegan Chambray. He was part of the Pointe-au-Chien Native American tribe and his family's ties to the cove and surrounding bayou went back generations, before the first American settlers.

Although K-Gee was two years older than Vashti and Bryce, they'd hung together while growing up. When Vashti had returned to town after losing her baby, K-Gee would walk Vashti and Bryce home from school every day. Even though Bryce never said, Vashti suspected something happened between Bryce and K-Gee during the time Vashti was away at that unwed home in Arkansas.

"When did K-Gee move back to Catalina Cove, Bryce?"

"Almost two years ago to help out his mom and to take over his family's seafood supply business when his father died. His mother passed away last year. And before you ask why I didn't tell you, Vash, you know

why. You never wanted to hear any news regarding what
was happening in Catalina Cove."

No, she hadn't, but anything having to do with K-Gee
wasn't just town news. Bryce should have known that.
"I'm sorry to hear about his parents. I really am. I'm
surprised he's on the zoning board."

For years the townsfolk of the cove had never recognized members of the Pointe-au-Chien Native American
tribe who lived on the east side of the bayou. Except for
when it was time to pay city taxes. With K-Gee on the
zoning board that meant change was possible in Catalina Cove after all.

"I need to know what you want to do, Vash," Bryce
said, interrupting her thoughts. "The Barnes Group is
giving us twenty days to finalize the deal or they will
withdraw their offer."

Vashti stood up to cross the kitchen floor and put
her teacup in the kitchen sink. "Okay, I'll think about
what you said. Ten million dollars is a lot of money."

"Yes, and just think what you could do with it."

Vashti was thinking and she loved all the possibili-
ties. Although she loved her job, she could stop working and spend the rest of her life traveling to all those
places her aunt always wanted to visit but hadn't, because of putting Shelby by the Sea first. Vashti wouldn't
make the same mistake.

THE NEXT MORNING, for the first time in two years, Vashti
woke up feeling like she was in control of her life and
could finally see a light—a bright one at that—at the
end of the road. Scott was out of her life, she had a great

job, but more importantly, some developer group was interested in her inn.

Her inn.

It seemed odd to think of Shelby by the Sea as hers when it had belonged to her aunt for as long as she could remember. Definitely long before Vashti was born. Her parents' home had been a mile away, and growing up she had spent a lot of her time at Shelby; especially during her teen years when she worked as her aunt's personal assistant. That's when she'd fallen in love with the inn and had thought it was the best place in the world.

Until…

Vashti pushed the "until" from her mind, refusing to go there and hoping Bryce was wrong about her having to return to Catalina Cove to face off with the rezoning board. There had to be another way and she intended to find it. Barely eighteen, she had needed to escape the town that had always been her safe haven because it had become a living hell for her.

An hour later Vashti had showered, dressed and was walking out her door ready to start her day at the Grand Nunes Luxury Hotel in Manhattan. But not before stopping at her favorite café on the corner to grab a blueberry muffin and a cup of coffee. Catalina Cove was considered the blueberry capital in the country, and even she couldn't resist this small indulgence from her hometown. She would be the first to admit that although this blueberry muffin was delicious, it was not as good as the ones Bryce's mother made and sold at their family's restaurant.

With the bag containing her muffin in one hand and

her cup of coffee in the other, Vashti caught the elevator up to the hotel's executive floor. She couldn't wait to get to work.

She'd heard that the big man himself, Gideon Nunes, was in town and would be meeting with several top members of the managerial and executive team, which would include her.

It was a half hour before lunch when she received a call to come to Mr. Nunes's office. Ten minutes later she walked out of the CEO's office stunned, in a state of shock. According to Mr. Nunes, his five hotels in the States had been sold, including this one. He'd further stated that the new owner was bringing in his own people, which meant her services were no longer needed.

In other words, she'd been fired.

CHAPTER TWO

A week later

VASHTI GLANCED AROUND the Louis Armstrong New Orleans International Airport. Although she'd never returned to Catalina Cove, she'd flown into this airport many times to attend a hotel conference or convention, or just to get away. Even though Catalina Cove was only an hour's drive away, she'd never been tempted to take the road trip to revisit the parish where she'd been born.

Today, with no job and more time on her hands than she really needed or wanted, in addition to the fact that there was ten million dollars dangling in front of her face, she was returning to Catalina Cove to attend the zoning board meeting and plead her case, although the thought of doing so was a bitter pill to swallow. When she'd left the cove she'd felt she didn't owe the town or its judgmental people anything. Likewise, they didn't owe her a thing. Now fourteen years later she was back and, to her way of thinking, Catalina Cove did owe her something.

COMING NEXT MONTH FROM

⬥ HARLEQUIN®

Desire

Available December 4, 2018

#2629 HIS UNTIL MIDNIGHT
Texas Cattleman's Club: Bachelor Auction • by Reese Ryan
When shy beauty Tessa Noble gets a makeover and steps in for her
brother at a bachelor auction, she doesn't expect her best friend,
rancher Ryan Bateman, to outbid *everyone*. But Ryan's attempt to
protect her ignites a desire that changes everything...

#2630 THE RIVAL'S HEIR
Billionaires and Babies • by Joss Wood
World-renowned architect Judah Huntley thought his ex's legacy would
be permanent trust issues, not a baby! But when rival architect
Darby Brogan steps in to help—for the price of career advice—playing
house becomes hotter than they imagined...

#2631 THE RANCHER'S SEDUCTION
Alaskan Oil Barons • by Catherine Mann
When former rodeo king Marshall is injured, he reluctantly accepts the
help of a live-in housekeeper to prepare his ranch for a Christmas
fund-raiser. But soon he's fighting his desire for this off-limits beauty,
and wondering what secrets Tally is hiding...

#2632 A CHRISTMAS PROPOSITION
Dallas Billionaires Club • by Jessica Lemmon
Scandal! The mayor's sister is marrying his nemesis! Except it's just
a rumor, and now the heiress needs a real husband, fast. Enter her
brother's sexy best friend, security expert Emmett Keaton. It's the perfect
convenient marriage...until they can't keep their hands to themselves!

#2633 BLAME IT ON CHRISTMAS
Southern Secrets • by Janice Maynard
When Mazie Tarleton was sixteen, J.B. Vaughan broke her heart. Now
she has him right where she wants him. But when they're accidentally
locked in together, the spark reignites. Will she execute the perfect
payback, or will he make a second chance work?

#2634 NASHVILLE REBEL
Sons of Country • by Sheri WhiteFeather
Sophie Cardinale wants a baby. Best friend and country superstar
Tommy Talbot offers to, well, *help* her out. But what was supposed to
be an emotions-free, fun fling suddenly has a lot more strings attached
than either of them expected!

**YOU CAN FIND MORE INFORMATION ON UPCOMING HARLEQUIN® TITLES,
FREE EXCERPTS AND MORE AT WWW.HARLEQUIN.COM.**

HDCNM1118

SPECIAL EXCERPT FROM

⬡ HARLEQUIN®

Desire

*Scandal! The mayor's sister is marrying his nemesis!
Except it's just a rumor, and now the heiress needs
a real husband, fast. Enter her brother's sexy
best friend, security expert Emmett Keaton. It's the
perfect convenient marriage... until they can't keep
their hands to themselves!*

Read on for a sneak peek of
A Christmas Proposition *by Jessica Lemmon,
part of her Dallas Billionaires Club series!*

His eyes dipped briefly to her lips, igniting a sizzle in the air that
had no place being there after he'd shared the sad story of his past.
Even so, her answering reaction was to study his firm mouth in
contemplation. The barely there scruff lining his angled jaw. His
dominating presence made her feel fragile yet safe at the same time.

The urge to comfort him—to comfort herself—lingered. This
time she didn't deny it.

With her free hand she reached up and cupped the thick column
of his neck, tugging him down. He resisted, but only barely, stopping
short a brief distance from her mouth to mutter one word.

"Hey…"

She didn't know if he'd meant to follow it with "this is a bad
idea" or "we shouldn't get carried away," but she didn't wait to find
out.

Her lips touched his gently and his mouth answered by puckering
to return the kiss. Her eyes sank closed and his hand flinched against
her palm.

He tasted…amazing. Like spiced cider and a capable, strong, heartbroken man who kept his hurts hidden from the outside world.

Eyes closed, she gripped the back of his neck tighter, angling her head to get more of his mouth. And when he pulled his hand from hers to come to rest on her shoulder, she swore she might melt from lust from that casual touch. His tongue came out to play, tangling with hers in a sensual, forbidden dance.

She used that free hand to fist his undershirt, tugging it up and brushing against the plane of his firm abs, and Emmett's response was to lift the hem of her sweater, where his rough fingertips touched the exposed skin of her torso.

A tight, needy sound escaped her throat, and his lips abruptly stopped moving against hers.

He pulled back, blinking at her with lust-heavy lids. She touched her mouth and looked away, the heady spell broken.

She'd just kissed her brother's best friend—a man who until today she might have jokingly described as her mortal enemy.

Worse, Emmett had kissed her back.

It was okay for this to be pretend—for their wedding to be an arrangement—but there was nothing black-and-white between them any longer. There was real attraction—as volatile as a live wire and as dangerous as a downed electric pole.

Whatever line they'd drawn by agreeing to marry, she'd stepped way, way over it.

He sobered quickly, recovering faster than she did. When he spoke, he echoed the words in her mind.

"That was a mistake."

Don't miss what happens next!
A Christmas Proposition by Jessica Lemmon,
part of her Dallas Billionaires Club series!

Available December 2018 wherever
Harlequin® Desire books and ebooks are sold.

www.Harlequin.com

Love Harlequin romance?

DISCOVER.

Be the first to find out about promotions, news and exclusive content!

Facebook.com/HarlequinBooks

Twitter.com/HarlequinBooks

Instagram.com/HarlequinBooks

Pinterest.com/HarlequinBooks

ReaderService.com

EXPLORE.

Sign up for the Harlequin e-newsletter and download a free book from any series at **TryHarlequin.com.**

CONNECT.

Join our Harlequin community to share your thoughts and connect with other romance readers!
Facebook.com/groups/HarlequinConnection

HARLEQUIN®

**ROMANCE WHEN
YOU NEED IT**

HSOCIAL2018